Dangerous Ride Across Humboldt Flats

Crossway Books for Young People by Stephen Bly

THE NATHAN T. RIGGINS WESTERN ADVENTURE SERIES

The Dog Who Would Not Smile
Coyote True
You Can Always Trust a Spotted Horse
The Last Stubborn Buffalo in Nevada
Never Dance with a Bobcat
Hawks Don't Say Goodbye

THE LEWIS AND CLARK SQUAD ADVENTURE SERIES

Intrigue at the Rafter B Ranch
The Secret of the Old Rifle
Treachery at the River Canyon
Revenge on Eagle Island
Danger at Deception Pass
Hazards of the Half-Court Press

RETTA BARRE'S OREGON TRAIL

The Lost Wagon Train
The Buffalo's Last Stand
The Plain Prairie Princess

ADVENTURES ON THE AMERICAN FRONTIER

Daring Rescue at Sonora Pass
Dangerous Ride Across Humboldt Flats
Mysterious Robbery on the Utah Plains

Adventures on the American Frontier ★ Book 2

Dangerous Ride

across Humboldt Flats

Stephen Bly

CROSSWAY BOOKS

A DIVISION OF
GOOD NEWS PUBLISHERS
WHEATON, ILLINOIS

Dangerous Ride Across Humboldt Flats

Published by Crossway Books
a division of Good News Publishers
1300 Crescent Street
Wheaton, Illinois 60187

Cover design: David LaPlaca

Cover illustration: Vito DiAngi

First printing, 2003

Printed in the United States of America

Library of Congress Cataloging-in-Publication Data

Bly, Stephen A., 1944 -
Dangerous ride across Humboldt Flats / Stephen Bly.
p. cm.
ISBN 1-58134-472-4 (TPB)
[1. Pony express—Fiction. 2. Orphans—Fiction. 3. Frontier and pioneer life—Nevada—Fiction. 4. Christian life—Fiction. 5. Nevada—History—19th century—Fiction.] I. Title. II. Series.
PZ7+
[Fic]—dc22 2003010616

DP 13 12 11 10 09 08 07 06 05 04 03
15 14 13 12 11 10 9 8 7 6 5 4 3 2 1

"For whosoever shall do the will of my Father
which is in heaven,
the same is
my brother, and sister, and mother."

MATTHEW 12:50 (KJV)

Author's Note

Although it has been over 140 years since the Pony Express thundered across the unsettled West, the stories about it still capture the hearts and imaginations of all Americans. It took bold businessmen like Russell, Majors, and Waddell to attempt such a feat without government subsidies. It would spell financial ruin for each of them.

It took a daring breed of men to be pony-riders (as they were called). They weighed 125 pounds or less. They carried a ball-and-cap pistol, a knife, twenty pounds of mail, and the prayers of a nation that searched the newspapers daily to read of their daring adventures. The pay was very good, but no man rode for the money. It was the thrill of fast horses, constant danger, and most of all, making history. The pony-riders and the country knew that this was a historic undertaking. Most of the incredible stories of their courage and stamina are true. Western heroism became an everyday news item in those turbulent months before the onslaught of the Civil War.

But rider and owner alike knew the Pony Express was temporary. It was meant to fill the gap between the slow mail service of Butterfield's southern route and the completion of the telegraph line. While no one thought it would last forever, many assumed it would last longer than eighteen months. A year and a half after its historic first run, the Pony Express was gone. But just as in 1860 and 1861, it lives on in our national heritage and pride. It is a part of who we are.

The Pony Express was not the first time horse relays had been used on a systematic basis to deliver news. The Romans used a horse relay, and in the thirteenth century, Kublai Khan employed 200,000 horses in message relays in Asia. But it is the Pony Express that lives on in the memories of Americans. It captured, not in myth but in reality, the wide open West that beckoned our entire nation and that summons many of us still.

Stephen Bly
Winchester, Idaho
Spring of 2003

ONE

November 10, 1860, near Humboldt Flats, Nevada Territory

Gabriel Young couldn't remember the last time he had a bath.

He knew he had one on Christmas Eve, but after that most days blurred like the shimmering horizon of northern Nevada as he rode west. The yellow-brown horse plodded without conviction.

Gabriel's shoulders slumped.

His stomach growled.

"Let's head back up to the river, boy." He patted the horse on the neck. "Even that muddy water will be better than an empty belly."

The high desert clumps of brown prairie grass contrasted with the gray-green sagebrush. Twelve inches deep, a hundred feet wide and muddy, the treeless Humboldt River meandered across the level basin. He slid off the horse and walked him to the edge of the river.

The horse balked at getting a drink.

"I know it ain't good. I know it's muddy. I know it tastes funny. I know it gives us both a stomach ache. But we don't have no choice. Here we are, big boy. God help us."

Gabriel pulled off his filthy shirt and splashed water on his face. He tried to scrub his arms, but the water rolled off the caked dirt at the bends of his elbows. After a gritty drink, he walked the horse away from the river. He tied the reins to his wrist and dropped to the dirt, his head on a clump of prairie grass. His sweat-soaked shirt hung from the saddle horn.

This isn't good. There are rodents that live better than this. The man said there was a mining camp at Chocolate Butte, but I can't even find the mountain. I should have stayed in Missouri . . . or Kansas . . . or Colorado . . . or Utah . . . well, maybe not Utah. I'll just rest here a minute or two. I need to keep lookin'. I'm too hungry to sleep.

"Hey, are you dead?"

Gabriel leaped to his feet. The horse shied back, tugging the reins at his wrist. "Wh-where did you come from?" he stammered.

A girl straddled a buckskin horse. Her gray skirt flowed across the saddle horn and almost down to her stirrups. "I guess you aren't dead."

Gabriel rubbed his eyes. "Where did you come from?"

"You're very dirty."

He glanced down at his bare arms and chest. "Where's my shirt?"

"If you mean that wretched yellow rag, it's over there in the dirt."

He grabbed up the shirt. "It ain't yellow. It's white."

"That shirt hasn't been white in a long time," she insisted.

"Don't look at me."

"You're filthy. Why would I want to look at you?"

He pulled the shirt over his head. "I've been on the trail awhile. Where did you come from?"

"You really ought to take better care of yourself. I've seen boys without their shirts on."

Gabriel's shirt felt wet and sticky. "Well, you ain't seen me. Where did you come from?"

"My mother says cleanliness is next to godliness. You need a bath."

"My mother's dead."

"I'm very sorry about your mother, but you're not honoring her memory when you don't take better care of yourself. You should put on a clean shirt."

Gabriel scanned the basin. No trees. No cabins. No wagons. Nothing but a raven-haired girl with a yellow-and-gray bonnet.

And a scowl.

"I don't own another shirt," he murmured. "I asked you, where did you come from?" He let the shirt hang out over his ducking trousers.

"What is your horse's name? My horse is Cedric."

"I don't reckon this horse has a name."

"Of course he does," she insisted. "When you talk to him, what do you call him?"

"I call him big boy, but that ain't his name."

"Yes, it is. Big Boy looks hungry."

"We're both sort of hungry, I reckon. Where did you come from?"

"When was the last time you fed Big Boy?"

"The same time I ate—yesterday mornin'. At least I think it was yesterday mornin'."

"You neglect meals too? I don't know how you can survive."

"I've been wonderin' the same thing myself."

"Mother's cooking cabbage for dinner, but I don't like

cabbage much. The ham will be tasty though. Do you like cabbage?"

"Right now I'd eat a cactus if I could pull off the spines. Where did you come from?"

"My mother makes jelly from prickly pear cactus."

He glanced at his dirty fingernails, then scratched the back of his neck. "Why won't you answer my question? Where did you come from?"

"I suppose we all come from God. After all, He shaped and formed us."

Gabriel pulled himself up into the saddle. "I wasn't askin' a theological question."

"My family is originally from East Alton, Illinois. That's just across the river from St. Louis, you know."

Gabriel studied her pale green eyes and upturned nose. "I don't care where you were born," he muttered. "When you rode up here, where did you come from?"

"Why do you want to know?" she demanded.

"I've been lookin' for two days for a minin' camp at a place called Chocolate Butte. I thought maybe you were from there."

She burst out in laughter.

"What's so funny?"

"You're looking for a mining camp at Chocolate Butte? There's no camp there."

"You mean, it's all played out?"

"I mean, there never was a camp. It's a hoax. Just one of the many prospectors' rumors."

"But I know it's there. I talked to a man in Jacumba who said he knew a man at Chocolate Butte who found color."

"No, it's not there. I made up that rumor."

"You what?"

"Cedric and I were playing a game one day about an imaginary gold mine at Chocolate Butte. Some men overheard me and believed it was real."

"Who's Cedric?" he asked.

"My horse. I told you that. Don't you listen to anything?"

"So there's no camp at Chocolate Butte?"

"Nope. You don't look like a prospector."

"I was lookin' for a camp job."

"You came to a barren place to look for a job."

"I'm on my way to California, sort of," he mumbled.

"By yourself?"

"No, I thought I'd take Big Boy with me."

"Big Boy?" she asked.

"My horse. Don't you listen to what I say?"

"Why are you going to California?"

"To find a job."

"And a bath, I trust."

"Are you goin' to tell me where you came from? Is there a town nearby? I really need a job."

"My mother's been to California. She says it's very pretty, and they can grow cherries. Wouldn't it be wonderful to have a cherry tree?"

"This conversation is goin' nowhere." He tipped his hat. "Good-bye. I need to find a town."

"My father's been to Mexico with General Scott. Have you ever been to Mexico?" she called out.

He rode away from the river. She trailed her horse behind him.

"No, I've never been to Mexico," he muttered and kept riding.

"Did your daddy fight in the Mexican War?"

"My daddy is dead."

"I'm sorry. How did your parents die?"

"Where did you come from?"

They rode along without speaking for several moments.

"You're going the wrong direction," she finally said.

"How can I be going the wrong direction? I don't even know where I'm headed. I'm goin' to whatever is this way."

"That will take you to Black Rock Desert and the Paiute Indians. You ever hear about the Paiute Indian War?"

"I don't guess so."

"You'll learn about it firsthand if you ride that direction for a day or two."

"You think they'd kill me?"

"Or worse."

"Worse? What's worse than dyin'?" he asked.

"I'm not sure, but my daddy says there are worse things than dyin'."

Gabriel rubbed his ribcage. "Yeah, sometimes livin' is worse than dyin'."

"That's very melancholy."

"It ain't been a happy day. What direction would you suggest I head?"

"I think south would be nice."

He turned the horse to the left and continued to plod across the high desert basin. "Why are you following me?"

"I can go anywhere I want."

"How old are you?"

"You don't know me well enough to ask that question," she scolded.

"I know you well enough to know that you're the youngest of the family and have older brothers."

"How did you know that?"

"'Cause you said you saw boys with their shirts off. That means you have brothers. And you're a pill, which means you're the baby of the family."

"That—that's very insulting."

"Was it true?"

"That's beside the point. You have no business talking to me like that."

"Then why don't you ride away?"

"Big Boy, is he always so surly? I don't know how you put up with him."

"Now you're talkin' to my horse?"

"Big Boy, would you please tell him that a smile and an ounce of pleasantness will often bring tenfold results over a scowl."

"You want me to smile?"

"Big Boy, tell him that it's difficult for me to stay cheerful in his presence."

"Cedric, did you know that the girl on your back has lost all sanity? I fear your safety could be in jeopardy if you continue to follow her lead."

She burst out laughing and clapped her hands.

"Cedric, would you ask her why she's laughing?"

"Big Boy, tell him I'm laughing because I got him talking to my horse."

He looked at her and grinned.

"Oh, yes! See, I knew you could smile!"

"You do act quite strange."

"That's because I'm the baby of the family and have three older brothers."

"I knew it!" he shouted.

"It was a lucky guess. Do you know their names?"

"Matthew, Mark, and Luke."

Her mouth dropped open, and she stared at him.

"You mean, I got it right?" he gasped.

"No," she grinned. "I just stared like that to see your reaction."

"You're really strange!"

"Will, Byron, and Keats."

"What?"

"My brothers are Will, Byron, and Keats."

"If I keep ridin' this direction, what will I find?"

"Humboldt Flats."

"I thought this whole area is Humboldt Flats."

"It is."

"Maybe you aren't real. Maybe I'm imaginin' all this. You're so vague, like a dream where everything is blurred."

"So you're saying that you find me dreamy?"

"I didn't say that."

"Then perhaps I'm a nightmare."

"That would be closer."

"Why do you keep insulting me?"

"How can I insult you? I don't even know who you are."

"I have a name."

"Are you goin' to tell it to me or just ignore me?"

"Only if you smile."

"What?"

"Smile for me again."

"This is crazy."

"Are you going to smile?"

He flashed a quick smile.

She clapped her hands. "That was very nice. Grubby, but nice. I'm Polk Lovelock."

"What?"

"My name is Polk Lovelock."

"Polk?"

"Daddy named me after the president."

He tipped his hat. "Nice to meet you, Polk. I'm Gabriel Young."

"Were you named after the angel?"

"I doubt it. My parents didn't live long enough for me to ask them."

"How did your parents die?"

"In a train wreck when I was three."

"Were you in the train with them?"

"Yep."

"Oh, I'm so sorry. I just don't know why things like that happen."

"Neither do I," he murmured.

"I wish I hadn't teased you," she admitted. "You're right. I can be a pill sometimes."

"Polk Lovelock, where did you come from when you rode up to the river?"

"Humboldt Flats Station."

"Station?"

"It's a Pony Express swing station. I live there with Mama and Daddy."

"Where is it?"

"Just over the next rise . . . about a mile away."

"Do you reckon there's any chores I could do for dinner and some hay for my horse?"

"You'll have to ask my daddy about chores. Mama will give you a meal. She never turns anyone away. As for the hay, I'll feed Big Boy myself. Me and him are pals."

TWO

"You'd better go ahead. I'll follow you," Gabriel suggested.

"Eh, no, you stay up there. I'll follow."

"But I don't know where the station is."

"You can't miss it over the next rise. It's the only building in sight. Right at the poplar trees."

He leaned his hand on the horse's rump and glanced back at her. "I don't know why you want to ride back there."

"Because the wind is at our backs."

"I smell that rank, huh?"

"Yes."

"I guess I'm too tired and hungry to care much."

"You shouldn't be alone out on the prairie."

"Neither should you."

"This is my home. Besides, Cedric is faster than any other horse. He's a Pony Express horse, you know."

"Big Boy used to be fast. But right now I reckon he's goin' at top speed."

They crested the next rise in the desert floor. Gabriel spotted a clump of trees about a mile south.

"Is that your place?"

"It belongs to Russell, Majors, and Waddell, but that's where I live."

"Just you and your folks?"

"And from time to time one of the riders spends a night. That's only if there's trouble. We aren't a home station."

"Sounds isolated."

"Not as isolated as riding across Nevada by yourself."

"What are those mountains over to the east?"

"The Humboldt Range. Chocolate Butte is about seven miles south of them."

"There really is such a place? I thought maybe you made up that name too."

"Nope."

"Is your name really Polk? I never knew a girl named Polk."

"And don't call me Poke or Pokey. Can I call you Gabe?"

"Sure."

"Look! Do you see that trail of dust? It's Hummer McGuire."

"Is he a pony-rider?"

"Yes, and he's very good. He knows how to play the bugle."

"I thought all the riders had to bugle the station as they approached."

"No, not anymore. We just listen for the hooves. But Hummer can actually play tunes on it, not just blast."

"If I was old enough, I might try to get one of the Pony Express jobs."

"They don't hire just anyone."

"I don't reckon I'm just anyone."

"Let's count when he hits the trees," she suggested.

"Count what?"

"Count how long it takes for him to change horses and reset his mochila."

"His what?"

"The saddlebags that hold the mail. Ready? One . . . two . . ."

"It surely seems like a lot of work to deliver some letters."

"Seven . . . eight . . . The mail is very important, and having a line of communication between the East and West benefits every person in our country. . . . nineteen . . . twenty . . ."

"That sounds like a memorized line."

"Twenty-four . . . It was. . . . twenty-six . . ."

"I heard they're considerin' puttin' in a telegraph line and that one day the Pony Express won't be needed."

"Thirty-two . . . thirty-three . . . I don't think the company is doing very well. I hear Mama and Daddy talk about going to California when it all folds up. Forty . . . forty-one . . ."

"You got kin in California?"

"Forty-three . . . forty-four . . . No, but Daddy says there's goin' to be a war back east. He doesn't want us to have to see it. . . . fifty . . . fifty-one . . ."

"You really think they'll go to war? I mean, I know a lot of 'em don't like Mr. Lincoln, but will they kill each other?"

"Fifty-eight . . . fifty-nine . . . Daddy thinks they will if Mr. Lincoln gets elected. One minute and one, two, three . . ."

"I've been too busy to follow the news much. I don't read all that good anyway."

"One minute and nine, ten . . . A person must always keep up with the news. Daddy says it's our duty as citizens to care about what happens in the world. . . . seventeen . . . eighteen . . ."

"Ever since Christmas I've just mainly been tryin' to stay alive. I reckon politics can take care of itself."

"Twenty-six . . . twenty-seven . . . Do you like being out on the prairie all by yourself? . . . thirty-two . . . thirty-three . . ."

"There he goes!" Gabe pointed to the clump of trees.

"One minute and thirty-four seconds! That's good. The rule is that it has to be under two minutes to change horses."

"How many horses do you keep at the station?"

"Twelve."

They continued to ride south down a gradual slope across the barren wilderness. The only movement was the column of dust from the Pony Express rider. High clouds streaked across the pale blue sky. The breeze at Gabe's back felt cool and yet comfortable.

"Your shirt is ripped in the back."

He glanced over his shoulder. "Yeah, I got hit with a branch."

"Did Big Boy run you through some brush?"

"No. The woman who held the branch was aimin' for my head, but she missed."

"Why was she beating on you?"

"I don't want to talk about it."

"Do you have a gun?" she asked.

"Why do you ask a question like that?"

"Are you saying that's an improper question?" she asked.

"How come you always try to pin me down?"

"Gabriel Young, you have a habit of answering a question with a question, don't you?"

"Me? What about you?"

"Do you like me, Gabe?"

"Wh-what kind of question is that?" he stammered.

"You see? You never answer me."

"No, I don't have a gun. There I answered you."

"How about the other question?"

"You're embarrassing me," he protested.

"I think you're a very strange boy."

"And I think you're a very strange girl." He stood in the stirrups. "Is that your wagon in the trees next to the station house? It looks like a freight wagon."

"Some of the men who freight up to the mines stop by the station to rest their teams and get water. Sometimes they let us buy things. Mama says it's like going to the store, but the store comes to us. I hope he doesn't leave before we get there. I need some ribbon. I wonder if he has any. Can Big Boy trot?"

"No, I think I'll be lucky to get him there at all. Why don't you ride on? I can find my way in from here. I just need to take it slow."

"I'll tell Mama and Daddy you're stopping by."

"Tell your daddy that I'll work for my meal. I don't expect nothin' for free."

"I'll see you at Humboldt Flats, Gabe Young."

"Good-bye, Polk Lovelock. I'll . . ." She galloped out of range of his voice.

Gabe crawled off his horse and loosened the worn

cinch. "Might as well relax your belt, boy. I'll walk you in from here. I don't reckon either of us will die today if her parents are like she says. Did you ever hear of a girl named Polk?"

The dirt was desert dry. His worn brown boots kicked up dust as he hiked through the scattered foot-high sage-brush. He could feel the grit on his sockless bare feet as they rubbed against the hard leather soles.

I'm so tired. My body is tired. My mind is tired of worryin'. And my spirit . . . well, I reckon my spirit died a long time ago. Maybe at the train wreck. Maybe when Grandma died. Maybe in Missouri. Or Kansas. It was way back there. And after that it's just survive one day at a time.

On days like today I just want to lay down in the dirt and give up.

Her daddy's right.

There are worse things than dyin'.

Livin' without hope, for one.

Polk is a dandy name, but it don't fit her. She looks too prissy, too pale, to be a Polk. But she surely ain't livin' in a prissy place. Humboldt Flats. It ain't even very flat. She did have purdy green eyes. Mary Edith Mercado had pretty green eyes too. And she hated me.

At least now I have a tad bit of hope.

Hope of a meal and a tree to sleep under. That's more than I had an hour ago.

The first thing I'm goin' to buy when I get some money is a pair of socks. Thick cotton socks.

Money.

I been workin' for meals so long, I can hardly remember what money looks like.

Gabriel led the horse closer to the stand of poplars. The station was a cabin about thirty feet wide and twelve feet deep. It faced east, with a front door that led out to a single uncovered front step. Rough, unpainted wood siding wrapped the building, and sun-bleached gray shakes covered the roof.

Twenty feet behind the building was an identical-sized structure that was three-sided and used for a barn. Behind it corrals stretched out in all directions from the two dozen poplar trees.

"So your name is Big Boy, huh? I reckon there's a spring here. Had to be somethin' that caused them trees to grow. And if there's a spring, then maybe there's clear water. A drink of clean water would be good for both of us."

Gabe felt the scabbard of his hunting knife rub against his leg on the inside of his boot. He reached down to adjust it. *She didn't ask me if I toted a knife. I wonder if she carries a gun? That dress covered up the entire saddle. No tellin' what was under there. A girl livin' out here with her folks—no friends or school around—it must be lonesome.*

Some folks ain't cut out for lonesome.

And some don't have any choice.

He saw a woman come out of the front door of the cabin and hike to the back of the freight wagon.

"I reckon I do smell rank, Big Boy. I appreciate you never complainin' about it. Maybe I shouldn't just trudge right up on them. Let's swing around to the east and circle the corrals and come up from the south side. Maybe then they won't chase me off real quick. If they got soap to spare, I'll try some scrubbin'." He rubbed his fingers on the back of his neck and rolled up dirt beneath them.

He heard laughter from the freight wagon, but he could no longer see anyone since the trees blocked his view. The corrals were made of four rough-cut cedar planks for rails and six- to ten-inch logs for posts. Gabriel counted ten horses scattered among three corrals.

Big Boy tugged at the reins and pulled him along.

"You found yourself some pals? There's got to be a water trough. . . . There it is." Gabriel looped the reins over the saddle horn and slapped the horse's rump. "Go on, get yourself a drink."

With a whinny and a snort, Big Boy bolted for the water trough.

I didn't know he had that much energy left. I reckon we all hold a little back for that last kick.

The barn shielded the trough from the back of the freight wagon so that he couldn't see anyone, but he could hear voices. He strained to listen but couldn't pick up the conversation.

Gabriel stared down at the mossy water trough. Big Boy looked up, and his last drink slobbered out of his mouth and back into the water. Twigs, dead leaves, and bits of green algae floated in the water. Gabriel pulled his tattered red bandanna from his back pocket and dipped it in the water, wringing it dry with his hands and then resoaking it. After repeating the process several times, he rolled up the wet bandanna and draped it around the back of his neck. He could feel the water soak through his cotton shirt.

He scooped up a double handful of water and drank it down fast. The first gulp bound in his throat, but the second went down easier.

"What I'd really like to do is stick my feet in there, Big

Boy. I don't reckon they'd mind, but I'd better wait and ask. Are you ready to meet the people? Maybe if I stand at a distance, I won't look and smell so bad."

The four people at the back of the freight wagon were so busy inspecting merchandise that they didn't glance his way. He took a dozen steps, leading his horse, and then stopped to stare.

She looks just like a mama ought to look. Hair stacked neat, standing straight, lace collar dress, hands folded. He pushed his hat back and took the bandanna and wiped his forehead. It was now streaked with brown dirt. *I don't reckon most children have any notion of the treasures given to them. I don't remember Mama, and my memory of Grandma fades more ever'day.*

He could only see the back of a tall man with stovepipe boots on the outside of his wool trousers and leather braces over his white cotton shirt. His hair was trimmed neatly, and Gabriel reached up and tried to comb his own shoulder-length hair with his fingers. It felt oily, tangled, dirty.

I reckon I do look like I crawled out of a hole. It hasn't bothered me before; so I don't know why I feel so self-conscious. Maybe it's Polk. She's got to explain me to her folks. Makes me feel like a stray dog that some little girl brings home. Maybe they'll just toss me a little meat and bread at the back door, and I'll ride on. I'd be mighty grateful for even that.

Polk spotted him. "Oh, here's Gabriel, the boy I told you about."

All four turned to face him.

"Welcome to Humboldt Flats, son," the tall man called out.

"Gabriel, I'm Mrs. Lovelock. Dinner will be ready shortly, and we insist you eat with us."

"You!" the bearded freighter shouted. "What in Hades are you doin' here?"

"Poker Bob?" Gabriel stammered.

The heavyset teamster reached into the wagon and yanked out a shotgun. "I told you I'd shoot you if I ever saw you again."

Gabriel leaped up into the saddle as he heard the explosion of black powder and shot. He kicked the horse's flanks, and Big Boy galloped south. Glancing back over his shoulder, he could see Mr. Lovelock wrestle the gun from the bearded man.

One hundred yards west of the corrals he slowed the horse down. "Big Boy, I reckon we won't have any supper after all."

THREE

Gabriel slid down out of the saddle and stared back to the east. "I don't see anyone chasin' us, Big Boy. Poker Bob ain't goin' to chase us with a freight wagon. Mr. Lovelock grabbed his gun. I don't reckon he wants to waste a pony-rider's horse followin' some no-account kid."

The ground heat shimmered the air and the building. The light green yellowing leaves of the poplars seemed to be caught in a breeze.

But there was no breeze.

Gabriel hiked west, his horse in tow, with an occasional glance over his shoulder.

I should have asked her more questions. I should have found out where the next station is. Pony-riders go fifty or more miles a day, but they have to change horses before then. Twenty miles. Maybe sooner. Must be a stage stop someplace. We should find some shade and rest. The only shade I've seen for two days was back at the Humboldt Flats Station.

Gabriel grabbed both ends of the still damp bandanna and yanked it back and forth. It rubbed hard on the back of his neck. He stopped when his neck felt raw. Then he examined the dirty bandanna before he twirled it tight and draped it back on his neck. "I have one spot clean. But I don't reckon many will notice the back of my neck."

I should have hung back. I should have waited for them to finish with Poker Bob. Then I could have still been there in the shade. Mama Lovelock asked me to stay for supper. Ham and cabbage.

Gabriel licked his lips. They tasted salty and dirty.

I didn't even fill my empty water jug. I can't believe it. I've been livin' like this long enough to know better. That girl distracted me. This is dumb. If I had some shade to rest in, I could wait for dark and sneak back and fill the water jug.

Big Boy halted and pitched his ears forward.

Gabriel tugged his hat down in the front and studied the western horizon.

"It's an antelope, boy. A pronghorn. I reckon I could roast that entire animal if I could kill him. And if I had a fire."

I'd probably eat him raw.

I can't believe I thought that. I can't believe what's happening to me. I just don't care. I don't care what I look like. What I smell like. What I drink. What I eat. There's no one to impress. I wouldn't eat it raw in front of Polk. Or her mama or daddy. At least, not her mama.

He looped the reins over a short sagebrush and dropped to his knees, yanking his hunting knife out of his boot. He put the worn cherry-wood handle in his mouth and crept forward on hands and knees.

One step. Pause. Another step. Pause again. He crept closer to the pronghorn grazing on the short brown grass that sprouted on the north side of a large clump of sage.

Every time the animal raised its head, Gabriel froze.

Then he flopped down on his stomach in the dirt. The pronghorn was only fifty feet away. *There is no chance in the world of bringing him down. I'll need a miracle from heaven.*

Gabriel reached up to grab the knife from his mouth. The antelope bolted southwest.

"No!" He jumped to his feet and hurled the knife at the fleeing animal. His throw was twenty-five feet to the right of the pronghorn. Gabe watched the dust trail of the sprinting animal and heard a clanging sound as the knife tumbled out of sight.

"Big Boy, did I just throw my knife into the rocks? That's a fine miracle." He waved his fist at the heavens. "All I'm asking for is to eat! Is that too much to ask? You feed the sparrows! How about me?"

He dropped his head and hiked back to the brown horse. "I know, Big Boy," he mumbled. "I promised not to complain anymore. But nothin' goes right for me. Now I probably lost my knife. It's hard to imagine my life getting worse. That was stupid. I didn't have a chance in the world of bringing down an animal with a thrown knife. My mind is playing tricks on me."

Gabriel led the big horse to where the dirt faded into broken volcanic rock.

He dropped the reins to the dirt. "You wait here, boy. No reason to tear up your hooves on this jagged rock."

I think I'm starting to lose my mind. I'm not thinking clear. I wonder if this is what happens right before a person starves to death? I wonder if I'm dyin'. Does a person ever know they're dying? If I just laid down on the hot desert, would I ever wake up? I'm so tired, but I can't lay down on this jagged rock.

The dark brown and red volcanic rock stabbed at the soles of his feet as he crept out on it. "This is great," he mumbled. "I don't even see my knife."

At first it looked like black rock, then a shadow, and then a hole.

"Big Boy, there's a trench out here." He hiked out a little farther. "A deep trench in the volcanic rock."

Gabriel stood at the edge and stared down. It was only about four feet wide but dropped straight down twelve to fifteen feet.

"And a cave. . . . There's a cave on the west side . . . and my knife. . . . How do I get down to the bottom?" *I think it leads down the slope to the south. Maybe if I flanked around, I could hike back in there and get my knife.*

He traipsed back off the volcanic rock to the horse. "Big Boy, I just might have found us some shade. It's almost underground, but it's shade."

It took half an hour to locate the sandy entrance to the trench on the south edge of the lava rock.

"You might as well come with me, Big Boy. If there's any shade, we can share it."

The trail started to the west, then turned north as it deepened.

"Out there it just looks like a dry little creek bed."

The trail widened, and soon Gabriel dropped down below ground level. "I bet the Paiutes know about this. I hope they aren't down here." He found his knife on the decomposed lava rock that lined the bottom of the trail and cave.

"Okay, boy, the cave is only five feet high and maybe eight feet wide. It's not big enough for you, but you can stand right here and not have any sunlight until tomorrow."

Gabriel loosened the cinch and pulled the saddle off. He slipped the bit from Big Boy's mouth and took the warm wool saddle blanket and wiped down the horse's sweaty back. "We'll just rest here until it gets dark and then sneak back for some water."

The shade felt good on his skin, and the sand floor felt cool as he crawled back into the cave. He stretched out with the saddle for a pillow. *There's no breeze at all down here. That's good when the winter blusters in.*

He lay on his back with his hands across his narrow stomach, eyes closed.

I can't believe my good luck in finding shade. Poker Bob will never find me here. No one will. Not until the Paiutes come back.

I can't believe I'm happy to find a hole in the ground. I'm living in a hole in the ground. I don't want to be here. But I don't have anywhere I want to be.

I'm tired.

Really tired.

There are things worse than dying.

He woke up with his arm stretched over his eyes. When he pulled his arm down, he couldn't see anything at all. He reached out and felt cool sand in his fingers. His arms were cold; so he rubbed his shirtsleeves to warm them.

Then he closed his eyes and rolled over on his side. Sand had trickled through the hole in his shirt and now slid down his back.

The cave! I'm in a hole in the ground.

He crawled on his knees until he could see stars overhead and then stood up. "Big Boy, we're goin' back for that drink of water now." He felt the north end of the trench. "Where are you? You didn't wander off—there's no place to go. And why am I whispering?"

His hands traced the jagged edges of the lava rock trench.

"This isn't funny! Where are you?" he called out. *He's gone! My horse is gone! He wandered off. Someone stole him. He's lost. No. No. No. He was all I had left in the world. You can't have him. I can't . . . no, no, no!*

Gabriel spun around and crashed into big slobbery lips. In the dim starlight he spied huge brown eyes.

"Big Boy!" He threw his arms around the horse's neck and hugged him. "Okay . . . it's okay now. It's okay. We're goin' to saddle you up and go get water."

The sweat on his face felt cold as he led the horse up out of the trench and onto the Great Basin. "I hope I can find Humboldt Flats in the dark. I thought there was some moonlight. There was moonlight last night. Remember? Or was that the night before? Or last week? Maybe the clouds are covering the moon."

Out on the flat prairie, he pulled himself up into the saddle. "Let's go, boy. Let's go get a drink."

After an hour of riding, Gabriel yanked the horse to a halt. "I don't think it was this far. And I surely can't figure out how we can miss the trees even in the dark. There's nothing else out here. I'm really tired of this. Everything I decide is wrong. Every decision gets me in worse trouble."

He unbuckled the headstall from the horse and dropped the bit out of Big Boy's mouth. He draped the bridle over the narrow saddle horn. "Okay, boy, where do you want to go? I'm just along for the ride. Take us somewhere."

When he kicked the horse's flanks, Big Boy took three steps forward, paused, then turned north, and broke into a trot.

"You got more of a nap than I thought. I can't believe you're runnin'. You do this till mornin', and you'll be dead. Slow down. Do you know what you're doin'?"

The horse cantered up over a rise in the desert floor. "Whoa," Gabriel hollered. "I see a light! It's just a flicker. Maybe someone's campfire. Slow down, boy. We don't want to startle them. It could be Paiutes. It could be Poker Bob. Or worse. Slow down . . . whoa!"

Big Boy broke into a gallop.

"What're you doin'?" Gabriel shouted.

The light remained a distant flicker, but now the big brown horse thundered ahead. Gabriel jammed his hat down tight and clutched the saddle horn with both hands.

Maybe I should jump off. I would probably break my neck but not die. If I stay, what trouble will I get myself into? I should never have pulled that bit out of his mouth. Even when I decide not to decide, it's the wrong decision.

They raced through the night with the tiny flicker of light always on the dark horizon.

"There's somethin' up there, boy, but we don't need to scare it away. Slow down."

The next time he scanned the horizon, the light was gone.

"We lost it. Or they heard us and put out the fire. Now they're waiting for us in the dark. I told you this would happen."

I don't think I'll live through this night. Is this the way it ends? Out on the desert. Racing to destruction. Alone. Nobody knows. Nobody cares. And I can't do anything about it.

It's like my entire life.

I've never been able to do anything about it.

Big Boy slowed so quickly that Gabriel slid up on the horse's neck. He jumped out of the saddle and walked beside the horse, holding the stirrup.

"Are you gettin' tired, boy? Is that why you slowed? I read about horses that have a sudden burst of energy right before they die. Is that it? Are we both givin' up at the same time?"

The horse stopped, and Gabriel could hear the animal's labored breathing.

"Don't leave me now, boy. I told you not to run. I begged you to slow down."

Then there was a whinny fifty feet ahead of them.

"Another horse?" he whispered. Still tugging on the stirrup, Gabriel led Big Boy toward the sound of the other horse. "A corral? Are those trees? It's the station at Humboldt Flats. You did it. I can't believe you did it."

Big Boy pulled loose and trotted to the water trough.

But what was the light? I know I saw a light. Maybe there was a lantern in the house, but it didn't seem like a lantern. We followed a light that wasn't here. Maybe I just thought I saw it.

Gabriel washed his face in the cold water of the horse trough. Then he pulled his bandanna across the mouth of the water jug and let it filter out the sticks and debris as water dribbled into the canteen.

If I wake up Mr. Lovelock, he might think someone's

out here stealin' his horses. I could get shot just takin' water out of the horse trough.

When the canteen was full, he looped it over the saddle horn and left Big Boy by the trough. He hiked around the barn toward the back of the station.

There are no windows back here. I couldn't have seen a lantern. It was a ghost light. Or a miracle. Or maybe my imagination.

Something white caught his eye near the back door, and he hiked closer.

A towel? Maybe a shirt? A rag?

He crept closer.

It's a towel . . . a tray . . . a hurricane lantern . . . a candle. There was a light, a real light. Someone left a candle burnin' on the back step.

With slow precision, he lifted the white cloth. Gabriel squinted, but he couldn't tell what was underneath. He stuck his finger into something mushy, then pulled his hand back, and licked.

Cabbage! It's cabbage!

He felt around for a slice of ham and shoved it all in his mouth.

Mama Lovelock left me some supper. She really did. Maybe it was Polk. And they left a candle so I could find it. They were thinkin' about me. All the time I was in a hole in the ground, they were thinkin' about me.

He folded the towel and laid it next to the hurricane candle. Then he plucked up the tray and carried it back out to the water trough. He shoved a finger full of cabbage into his mouth as he walked along. When he got to the corral, Big Boy was munching on hay.

"They left you some hay, boy? They were thinkin' of

you too. You did it, boy. You brought us back. And the Lovelock family is feedin' us, no matter what Poker Bob told them. They're good people. Real good people."

Gabriel sat on the dirt, his back against a corral post, balancing the tray in his lap. He shoveled in the ham and cabbage with his fingers. There was something that tasted like beets, and the sweet taste of flaky crust and apples.

Mama Lovelock, that's the best apple pie I ever had in my life.

With his shirtsleeve, he wiped away the tears as he fingered another bite of pie. When every bite was gone, he held the plate up in the starlight and licked it until there was no more taste. His hands and mouth were sticky as he set the plate back in the wooden tray. Something metal rattled.

A knife and a fork? I ate supper with my dirty hands. I can't believe how good that tasted. Stone-cold, it was delicious.

Gabriel shoved the tray to the side and scooted over to the water trough where he washed his face and hands and tried to dry them off on his shirtsleeve. Then he crawled back over to the corral post and leaned against it as he sat on the dirt.

I'll just rest here until Big Boy is done. Then we'll slip on out. One day at a time, and I think we're goin' to survive this one after all.

"Hey, are you dead?"

Gabriel blinked his eyes open. Daylight streamed across northern Nevada, and Polk Lovelock stood in front of him, her arms crossed.

"That's the second time in two days that you asked me that," he replied.

"Daddy said that much food on an empty stomach might make you sick, but Mama said you looked at death's door and piled it on anyway."

"It was wonderful. I didn't mean to sleep here all night."

Mrs. Lovelock hiked out the back door. "How are you this morning, Gabriel?"

He leaped to his feet and tugged off his hat . . . and vomited all over the wooden tray.

FOUR

Mrs. Lovelock scrambled to Gabriel's side even as he still rested his hands on his knees. She tugged off her apron and wiped his face.

"I'm sorry, ma'am."

"Now that's okay, honey."

"You folks were good to me, and look what I've done."

"It's all right, Gabriel. It was my fault," Mrs. Lovelock comforted him.

"I can't believe I did that."

She patted him on the back. "Mr. Lovelock told us your stomach couldn't take that much. I just didn't believe him."

"I ain't throwed up in a long time, ma'am. Truly I ain't."

"Gabriel Young, would you quit apologizing long enough to listen to me?"

"Yes, ma'am."

"You didn't do anything wrong. No one is ever to blame for losing their supper or their breakfast. You wait right here. Let me bring you a basin of warm water so you can wash your face." She turned to Polk, who seemed to be frozen in place. "Sissy, you tote that tray and dishes into the house."

"Do I have to?" she gasped.

"Eh, no. I'll take them. You stay here and visit with Gabriel."

He wiped his mouth and chin on his shirtsleeve. "I surely appreciate the candlelight and food even though I couldn't keep it down."

"The supper was Mama's idea. She wanted Daddy to go after you, but he said we can't force a man to come back."

"He called me a man?"

"Yes, Daddy is very generous that way." Polk refused to look at him. She stared across the corral. "He said that if you were smart, you'd sneak back after dark and get some water. I told Mama you could have trouble findin' your way back, and we should set out a candle. Daddy said you couldn't see it if you went west, but I guess you did."

"I think I went south by mistake, but Big Boy brought me back until we saw the candle. I thought it was a sign from heaven at first."

"Maybe it was."

"No, it was just your candle."

"How do you know, Gabriel Young, that the Lord didn't use my candle as His sign?"

"I don't know nothin' about how the Lord works." He caught his breath and stood up straight.

She glanced at him, then turned away. "You simply must stay so I can tell you everything."

"Stay?"

"Yes. Daddy said he had some chores you could do,

unless you had somewhere else to go. Do you have anywhere else to go?"

"Eh, well . . . not for a while. I reckon I could stay and help your daddy." *A few months or maybe a year would be nice.*

"Did you really steal those things from Poker Bob?"

Gabriel gave up trying to get her to look at him. He gazed across at the horses. "Is that what he told you?"

"He said he tried to help you, and you stole him blind."

"That's a lie, but it's a long story. If that's what he told you, why is your family so nice to me?"

"Mama didn't believe him. To her you just looked like a half-starved boy, and she figures it's the Lord's will that she feed you."

"Your family is kind of religious, ain't they?"

"I don't know. Are we?" Polk shrugged her narrow shoulders.

Mrs. Lovelock hiked out to the barn with a porcelain bowl in one hand and towels over her shoulder. "Sissy, run get one of the pony-riders' buckskin shirts."

"Are you going to give him the shirt?"

"No person on earth should have to wear a shirt that he's vomited on," Mrs. Lovelock said.

Gabriel hiked over to the barn where Mrs. Lovelock had set the large basin.

"Here's some lye soap and a rag. Come wash yourself up."

"Mrs. Lovelock, you surely are treatin' me square, and you don't know anything about me."

"I'd guess you to be around thirteen."

"Fourteen," he corrected.

"A fourteen-year-old orphaned young man wanderin' aimlessly on a dangerous high desert of Nevada Territory just about to starve to death. Just how much more do I need to know?"

Polk skipped out carrying a pullover buckskin shirt over her arm. Her raven hair curled halfway down her back.

"I reckon you want to know my side of the story with Poker Bob," he said.

"Only if you want to tell us." Mrs. Lovelock handed him a rag.

Gabriel lathered up and started to wash his face. "I do want to tell you 'cause I want you to know what really happened, and I ain't had anyone to explain it to before. I was in Pine Bluff, Utah, a month or so ago. At least, I think it was a month. I sort of lost track of time."

"It was about 6:30 A.M. on Monday, November 12, 1860," Polk offered.

"Sissy, be still and let Gabriel finish."

Gabriel scrubbed his face and neck. "You see, Pine Bluff is just a minin' camp, and I was scoutin' around for odd jobs, workin' for meals mostly. Poker Bob pulled in with his wagons and asked me to help him unload. Said he would buy me supper and give me a new shirt. I asked for a pair of socks too, and he agreed."

"You missed a spot on the side of your neck. Would you like me to scrub there for you?" Mrs. Lovelock asked.

"Eh, yes, ma'am, if it ain't no bother."

"Sit down on this wooden keg."

Gabriel surrendered the soapy rag and plopped down. He felt the warm rag scrubbing his neck.

"Now please continue," Mrs. Lovelock urged.

"It was hard work unloadin' the wagons 'cause there was plenty of heavy mining equipment. He had tandem wagons and a dozen oxen pullin' them. After we finished the first wagon, he got thirsty and went off to find a drink. He said for me to go ahead and unload whatever I could from the second wagon till he got back. I unloaded the light stuff, but he still wasn't back; so I started unloading the heavier things."

"By yourself?"

"Yes, ma'am. I'm sturdier than I look."

"I imagine you are. Now lift your head up, Gabriel. Let me wash around front in just a place or two you missed. I'd better clean this rag first."

"Look how dirty that water is," Polk gasped.

"That's why we wash, dear. To get the dirt off. Now go on, Gabriel."

"Anyway, I saved the heaviest crate for last, but he still didn't show; so I tried slidin' it down the tailgate. It sort of slipped off and busted the crate. I'm sure it didn't bust the big ol' pulley inside, but the crate was splintered."

"Close your eyes," Mrs. Lovelock said.

"Yes, ma'am."

She scrubbed his forehead and around his eyes.

"I don't reckon I ever had anyone clean me up before except my grandmother. At least I don't remember."

"What did Poker Bob do about the broken crate?" Polk asked.

"When he didn't come back, I went lookin' for him. I found him in a . . . well, it was a . . ."

"A saloon?" Mrs. Lovelock asked.

"Yes, ma'am. Just a big ol' tent actually."

"You went into a saloon?" Polk asked.

"I been in a lot of places I ain't proud to mention. But I was hungry and had a meal comin'. Anyway, Poker Bob had downed several drinks and was playin' cards in the corner with three prospectors and some dandy in a silk top hat."

"Did he buy you a meal?" queried Polk.

"Yep, he bought me a chop and some potatoes and a piece of apple pie. It was a fine meal for a hungry boy, but the pie didn't hold a candle to yours, ma'am."

"Thank you, Gabriel. I trust it wasn't the pie that made you sick at your stomach."

"Did you get your socks and shirt?" Polk asked.

"When I asked Poker Bob about them, he said to wait until the card game was over."

"How long did that take?" Polk asked.

"I sat out in front of the saloon until midnight. By then Poker Bob had had several more drinks and lost a large sum of money to the dandy in the silk top hat."

"I don't suppose he was in a happy mood," Mrs. Lovelock said.

"No, ma'am. He wanted to wait until mornin' to get my goods, but I insisted on it right then. I didn't want him to wake up and not remember what he promised."

"What did he say about the busted crate?" Polk asked.

"He cussed me out and said I was sloppy and did a lousy job and didn't earn a shirt and socks."

"Poker Bob said that?" Mrs. Lovelock pressed.

"Yes, ma'am. Then he crawled up in the front wagon and went to sleep."

"So you took the shirt and socks?" Polk asked.

Gabriel sat up straight as Mrs. Lovelock dried his face

with a clean towel. "Yes, I did. I didn't think of it as stealin' but as pay that was due me. I did the very best I could without any help on the second wagon."

"So what did Poker Bob do the next mornin'?"

"I made the mistake of stayin' in camp overnight. I was down at the Chinese laundry helpin' them beat out some clothes when Poker Bob and a couple of his friends found me. They had guns pointed at me and made me pull off the shirt and socks. They ran me out of the camp barefoot, carryin' my boots."

"How about a shirt? Did you have a shirt?" Polk asked.

"Nope. I had thrown away my other one. Ching Chang, the man at the Chinese laundry—I don't reckon that was his real name, but that's what ever'one called him—sent his boy out with a shirt for me."

"Is that the one you're wearin' now?" Mrs. Lovelock asked.

"Yes, ma'am. Poker Bob said if he ever saw me again, he'd shoot me on sight."

"He won't shoot you here," Polk told him. "Daddy chased him off and won't let him come back."

"Really?"

"He said that no one was goin' to shoot at his guests."

"I did take his shirt and socks. I never thought of it as stealin'. I ain't never stole anything in my life except food, and that was only 'cause I got so hungry that I was thinkin' crazy."

"That's understandable," Mrs. Lovelock remarked. "You'll have no cause for stealing food around here. Russell, Majors, and Waddell supply each station with plenty of food."

"Are them the men that own the Pony Express?"

"Yes, but there seems to be some debate over which creditor will assume control."

"Business ain't doin' too good?"

"Daddy doesn't think it was ever meant to do good," Polk blurted out. "The Pony Express was started just to show that the central route is better for mail than the southern route."

"I thought it cost a lot to send a letter by pony-rider."

"Ten dollars an ounce," Polk said.

"Ten dollars? I ain't made dollars in a whole year. But I'm surely sorry about the company."

"We knew it was temporary. Mr. Lovelock figures another year is about all it will last."

"Daddy says that someday they'll have a railroad right through here."

"I don't guess I have much use for trains. They didn't do my mama and daddy much good."

"As long as you're scrubbing, you might as well wash those arms."

"Yes, ma'am, I reckon I should." He rolled up his shirtsleeves.

"Gabriel, pull off that old shirt and scrub up good," she instructed. "Sissy, you go in the house."

"Why?"

"Gabriel should not have to pull off his shirt in front of a young lady."

"I'm just a girl."

"Go in the house."

"I've already seen him with his shirt off."

"Polk Lovelock, you go in the house right now."

Polk stomped off, mumbling to herself.

"Now pull off your shirt, Gabriel."

He hesitated.

"Young man, I have three sons. I have overseen scrubbing up many a boy. Pull off your shirt."

"Yes, ma'am. Polk said their names are Will, Byron, and Keats."

"Mr. Lovelock allowed me to name the boys."

"And he named Polk?"

"Yes. He really wanted to name her Scott, but I said no girl on earth should be called Scott. Not that Polk is much better. That's why I call her Sissy."

"I think Polk is a bang-tail of a name. I like it."

"Please tell her that. She gets teased a lot. Now get that shirt off. And while you're scrubbing, you might want to pull off your—"

"In front of you?" he gasped.

She smiled. "I was going to say 'pull off your boots.' But you're right. You should wash all over. I'll go in the house and fix you some mush while you clean up. I think you better stick to very plain food until your stomach settles down."

"Yes, ma'am. I reckon you're right."

"Give me that shirt. I'll see if I can wash and mend it."

Gabriel dropped his suspenders to his sides and pulled his shirt off over his head.

"Oh, my word!" Mrs. Lovelock exclaimed.

He handed her the shirt. "What's the matter, ma'am? Did I do something wrong?"

"Look at your ribs."

"What's the matter with them?"

"I can count them all. Just skin and bones. Oh, honey . . ." Mrs. Lovelock began to sob.

"I'm sorry. Don't cry. You want me to put my shirt back on?"

"No . . . No, honey. . . . It's okay." She dried her eyes on her apron. "No child should be that hungry. No child. No one." She covered her mouth and started to sob again.

Several inches shorter than Gabriel, Virginia Lovelock threw her arms around his shoulders and hugged him tight.

He kept his arms down. "I'm still kind of dirty, ma'am."

"When was the last time you were hugged, Gabriel Young?"

"I don't reckon I remember."

"I don't care how dirty you are. Every boy needs a hug from a mama."

He slowly put his arms around her and clutched tight.

And sobbed.

FIVE

"Your face and neck look pink," Polk said when Gabriel ambled out of the barn.

"Your mama scrubbed off two years of dirt."

"That shirt looks nice on you."

"Thank you, Polk. I do believe it's the nicest shirt I ever wore."

"It used to belong to Billy McGuire, but when he quit pony-riding, he put on weight, and it doesn't fit anymore."

"I'm glad he did."

"Mama wants you to have these too."

"What are they?"

"Some of Daddy's old wool socks."

"Socks? I'll have to work until summer to pay you back for all of this."

"We're not selling them to you. We're giving them to you."

"I don't take gifts. I'll work for 'em."

"Why don't you let others help you? I suppose it's stubborn pride," she said.

"It ain't pride. It's just . . . it's just not right!"

"Daddy says everyone needs help sometimes, and

everyone should give help sometimes. He says it all balances out."

Gabriel sat down on a barrel in front of the barn and tugged at his boots.

"Do you want me to help pull your boots off?"

"I can take off my own boots," he insisted.

"I'm sure you can. So can my daddy, but he always lets my mama help him anyway."

"We ain't married."

"Oh, are you saying we have to be married before you'd let me help you with anything?"

"All I'm sayin' is, I can pull off my own boots."

"I believe it's stubborn pride."

"You aren't goin' to be happy until you pull off my boots, are you?"

Polk wrinkled her nose and grinned. "Nope."

Gabriel shoved a boot toward her. "I feel ridiculous."

She grabbed the heel and toe of his left boot. "That's silly. There's no one around for fifteen miles to see you."

She yanked so hard that it pulled him off the barrel, and he crashed to the dirt.

"Are you all right?" Polk stood over him, his boot in her hand.

Trent Lovelock hiked around the corner of the corrals. "What happened here?"

"I pulled off his boot, Daddy."

"Mr. Lovelock, I tried to tell her that I could pull them off by myself."

"He has a lot of stubborn pride," she smirked.

"I expect sittin' on the dirt, he has less of it now," Mr. Lovelock chuckled.

"Don't I get to pull off your other boot?" Polk asked.

Gabriel glanced at Mr. Lovelock.

"That's up to you, son. You think you can live through more help?"

"I lived through a tornado last spring out in Kansas; so I reckon I can live through Polk Lovelock." Gabriel grinned.

"You see, Daddy, I told you he had a fetching smile."

Gabriel shook his head. "I never in my life met anyone who embarrassed me more than this girl."

"Thank you. Now give me the other foot."

He sat down on the barrel and again stuck a foot out. Polk grabbed his heel and toe and yanked. This time he stayed on the barrel.

"Why are you pullin' off your boots?" Mr. Lovelock asked.

"Mama gave Gabe a pair of your old socks."

"Maybe he doesn't want to be called Gabe, darlin'. You don't like it when folks call you something different."

"Gabe is fine. My friends usually call me Gabe, you know, that is—when I have friends. I hope it's okay about the socks."

Mr. Lovelock glanced at the socks in Gabriel's hand. "No, it's not okay."

"Daddy!" Polk protested.

"I understand, sir." Gabriel swallowed hard and handed them to Mr. Lovelock.

"Polk, this is my oldest pair of socks. You run in the house and get Gabe that new pair of wool socks. I've been savin' them for something special, and now I know what."

"Oh, no, sir. I couldn't take them. I wouldn't feel right about wearin' 'em. Let me have the old ones."

"Daddy, I warned you—he's very stubborn."

Mr. Lovelock stared at his daughter's green eyes. "In that case . . ." He handed Gabriel the socks. "Of course, he's not the only one around here who is stubborn and prideful."

"Daddy doesn't mean it. He's just teasing." Polk handed Gabriel a boot. "You have holes in the soles of your boots."

"They aren't very big ones," he muttered.

"Polk, go get my leather-workin' kit by the front door."

"I ain't goin' to let you give me any boots. I just can't be that beholdin'. It ain't right."

"I understand pride, son. I'm not goin' to give you boots. But I can slip a piece of leather in there so your socks don't get dirty. Is that all right?"

"Yes, sir. I reckon it is."

Polk scampered to the house.

"Mr. Lovelock, you folks are treatin' me good, and I want to work it off. I'm not a thief, sir, no matter what Poker Bob said."

"Mama told me your side of the story, and I have no reason to doubt you, son."

Gabriel pulled the socks over his clean feet. "You know, Mrs. Lovelock is purtnear the sweetest lady I ever met in my life. When I dream about my mama, I always dream of a lady like her."

Mr. Lovelock glanced toward the back of the station house. "That lady's had a lot of testin', but the sweetness always wins out."

"What kind of testin'?" Gabriel asked.

"I took all my money from our Illinois farm and

bought a freight line into Colorado durin' the Pike's Peak gold rush."

"I heard that wasn't much of a strike."

"They played it up big. I lost my shirt in that deal. That's why we're out here at a little swing station like this. I'm trying to pay Mr. Majors back for dealing with my creditors."

"A swing station?"

"Home stations are where the pony-riders stay on their days off. There's twenty-six of them stretching from St. Joseph to Sacramento. But in between, every fifteen miles, is a swing station like this one, a place to relay the horses."

"How many of them are there?"

"They started out with 165, but as they build that telegraph line, some stations will be closing."

Polk stood on the back doorstep. "Daddy, your leather kit isn't by the front door."

"That's right. I had it out here with the saddles last evenin'. I'll fetch it, darlin'."

"Gabe, Mama says your breakfast is ready," Polk shouted. "Do you need help putting on your boots?"

"You go help Mama," Mr. Lovelock commanded.

"Daddy, I want to talk to Gabe."

"He'll be around awhile, darlin'. Go on back in the house."

When Polk sulked back into the house, Mr. Lovelock turned to Gabriel. "You are plannin' to stay awhile, aren't you? It would break Mrs. Lovelock's heart if you were to leave before she put some meat on your bones."

"I wouldn't do nothin' to hurt her. And I'm sorry about your freightin' business."

"Things come and go in life. I reckon we shouldn't clutch on to them too much. It's when people come and go that it's rough. Don't pull on them boots yet. Let me get that leather kit."

Gabriel studied the clouds that sailed high across the Great Basin. *Lots of times my life is like a bad dream. I keep hopin' I'll wake up and be someplace better. But now it seems like a good dream, and I'm afraid of wakin' up in some dark hole in the ground. I don't know why good things never last, and bad things you can't ever get rid of.*

"Here you go, Gabe," Mr. Lovelock said.

Gabriel shoved the thick brown leather insoles into his boots and slipped his feet in. He wiggled his toes.

"How does that feel?" Mr. Lovelock asked.

"Mighty good, Mr. Lovelock. Shoot, I could dance all night."

Mr. Lovelock stared at him a moment and then grinned. "Well, don't tell Mrs. Lovelock that. She has the idea that dancin' is the devil's tool."

"No, sir. I won't offend her for nothin'. Is there anything else I ought to know so that I don't offend her?"

"I don't know about offendin', son, but you'd understand her better if you knew about the babies she lost."

"Other children?"

"After the boys were born, she had a couple of painful miscarriages. Doctor said it was time to quit having children, but she couldn't accept that. Then about a year before Polk was born, we had another boy. He only lived a couple months. This time she believed the doc, and we decided no more children."

"And then Polk came along?"

"A total surprise from the Lord. Isn't that the way it usually happens? We give up, and the Lord takes over."

"I don't know much about the Lord, sir."

Polk peeked out the back door. "Daddy, you must simply stop droning on to Gabe and let him come eat before the mush gets cold."

"Now if you start understanding that daughter of ours, you'll be the only one who can. When you're through eating, come to the corrals. We'll hitch up a team and head to the Humboldts for some firewood."

Gabriel got up and headed for the back door. "Yes, sir, I'll be right back."

"Eat slowly this time, son."

"Yes, sir, I will."

Gabriel knocked at the back door of the station house.

"Come in," Mrs. Lovelock hollered.

He stuck his head through the doorway of the two-room station house. Mrs. Lovelock stood at the counter peeling potatoes. Polk sprawled on a wooden chair at the large table.

"Mama Lovelock, this is your home. I can't be bargin' in on you. I'm used to eatin' out on the back step. That's just fine with me."

"What did you call her?" Polk asked.

"Eh . . . Mrs. Lovelock?"

"No, you called her Mama Lovelock," Polk squealed.

Gabriel felt his face flush. "Ma'am, I'm sorry about that. I don't know how that—"

"It was very sweet," Mrs. Lovelock told him. "It would be an honor for you to call me Mama Lovelock.

Now wipe your feet and come in. No guest of mine eats on the back step. Ever. That's a Mama Lovelock rule."

Mr. Lovelock was trimming horse hooves when Gabriel traipsed out to the corrals.

"How are you feelin' now, son?"

"I'm hopin' to keep this meal down. I had me some mush and biscuits with cactus jelly and coffee. Right at the moment I'm feelin' mighty good. From now on, I aim to be up at the crack of dawn to help you out."

"Son, you get up when you want. Most times I can use the help around the middle of the day. That's when the pony-riders come through."

"They don't come through ever'day, do they?"

"Nope. Every other day. Tomorrow it's time for the westbound rider. Supposed to be election news. Sometimes east and west riders hit here on the same day. It just depends. We never know for sure. Can you hook up a team, son?"

"Yes, sir, I can."

"I knew you could. Took one look at you and said, 'That boy can handle a team.' Hook up those two bay mares to the wagon while I finish trimmin' these hooves. Those shoes on Big Boy were as worn as your boots. I pulled them and trimmed him up. I reckon you should let him rest up for a while."

"Yes, sir, I appreciate it. He's been with me for two years, and I'm sort of fond of him, as ugly as he might be."

"Son, a good horse isn't ever ugly."

Gabriel had just finished hooking up the team when Mr. Lovelock tossed axes and saws in the back of the wagon.

"How far do we have to go for wood?"

"About ten miles southeast of here in the Humboldt Range. That's as close as we are to timber."

Polk carried a basket, and Mrs. Lovelock brought a water jug out to them.

"There's some lunch in here if you get hungry," Mrs. Lovelock announced. "Trent, those extra biscuits are for my Gabe. I think they'll be good on his stomach; so don't you go eating them all."

"Daddy, I could go with you and Gabe if you want me to," Polk offered.

"You stay with your mother. She might need some help around here."

"You used to take me to get wood."

"That was when you were just a kid, Polk darlin'. Now that you're a young lady, a wood camp just isn't the place to take you."

"Daddy, are you trying to sweet-talk me into doing what I don't want to do?"

"Did it work?"

Polk flashed a wide, easy grin. "It worked this time, but don't you try it again."

Mr. Lovelock loaded the goods in the wagon. "You want to drive, son?"

"Yes, sir. I believe I do."

"You never let me drive to wood camp," Polk pouted.

"We'll try to be back right before dark. Polk darlin', you grain-feed the horses for me."

"I will, Daddy. Bye, Gabe."

Gabriel slapped the lead lines on the horse's rump, and as they turned, he tipped his slouch hat. "Bye, Polk. Good-bye, Mama Lovelock."

Mrs. Lovelock folded her arms across her blue gingham dress and smiled. "Good-bye, my Gabe."

They rattled and rolled about a mile before either spoke up.

"Did you hear her?" Gabriel asked. "She called me 'my Gabe.'"

"Son, let me tell you somethin' about that woman. Did you ever hear of the Gila monsters down in Arizona?"

"Them is big lizards, ain't they?"

"Sort of like that. But they can grow as big as a small dog. They got special jaws that lock up once they bite something."

"Lock up?"

"They don't let go. Mama Lovelock is like that. If she chooses to hold on to you, she isn't ever going to let go. You are now officially, until the last breath she breathes, 'her Gabe.' There isn't any way on earth you're ever going to get out of it."

Gabriel swallowed hard. He sucked in a breath of air. He fought it until his vision blurred. Then he gave in and wiped his eyes on his buckskin shirt.

"This old Nevada dust can surely tear up a man, can't it?" Mr. Lovelock commented.

"Yes, sir," Gabriel sniffed. "I reckon it can."

SIX

The high desert stretched west at a gradual incline to the base of the Humboldt Range. A narrow pass led up into the mountains.

"I don't see any trees," Gabriel said.

"Don't that beat all?" Mr. Lovelock yanked off his slouch hat and wiped his forehead. "From down here a person would say the whole land is desolate. But the pines are up there. Stop over there by the shade of that boulder. Let's rest the ponies before we climb up to the pines. I could use one of them biscuits. How about you?"

"Yes, sir. That sounds tasty." Gabriel parked the wagon and climbed down. "Your team is kind of small for pulling a wagon."

Mr. Lovelock handed him the basket and water jug and climbed down. "Yep, you're right, son. They're Pony Express horses. They won't buy one over fifteen hands. They want fast, grain-fed horses."

Gabriel dug through the basket and plucked out a biscuit. "Grain-fed?"

"Yep, they outrun those Indian ponies that feed on grass. They got more muscles and stamina. The pony-riders tell me their greatest defense against the Indians is that they can outrun them. They paid $200 to $300 a head for some of these horses." Mr. Lovelock took a swig of water and handed the jug to Gabriel.

Gabe took a swig and wiped his mouth on his sleeve. "I ain't never seen a $300 horse."

"There's two of them standing right there."

"No foolin'?" Gabriel mumbled through a mouthful of biscuit. "I only paid eight dollars for Big Boy. It wasn't cash dollars. I worked two weeks at a mill, and they gave him to me."

Mr. Lovelock pulled out a slice of salt pork and folded it inside a biscuit. "He's worth a whole lot more than eight dollars, isn't he?"

"Yes, sir, he is. I reckon that's why all the pony-riders are small, you havin' such short horses." Gabriel dug out some salt pork for his biscuit. "I surely hope this don't make me sick, but I'm hungry for meat."

"Give it a try, son, but don't overdo it. You're right—it takes a small man to be a pony-rider. The regulations are that we can only have 165 pounds on a horse. They got special saddles and tack that only weigh 25 pounds. The mail is about 20 pounds. So the men have to weigh around 120 pounds."

Gabriel took another big bite of biscuit and pork. "I reckon until Mama Lovelock fills me up, I'd probably qualify."

Mr. Lovelock gazed back across the Great Basin to the west. "I reckon you would."

"I seen an illustration in *Harper's Weekly* of a rider carryin' a carbine across his lap. They don't really carry carbines, do they?"

Mr. Lovelock dug through the basket. "Not anymore.

At first they were supposed to tote a bugle, carbine, and pistol. Nowadays the thundering hooves serve as a trumpet, and the revolver and knife are the only weapons. Some boys carry a loaded spare cylinder, of course. You want to split this sweet onion with me, son?"

"I reckon my stomach would be better off if I just passed on that." He took another swig of water. "Polk said there's Indian trouble farther west of here."

"It was bad. I suppose a dozen or more station tenders and helpers got killed."

"I heard the army settled things down."

"For a while." Mr. Lovelock scooped a couple of handfuls of oats from a sack under the wagon seat and fed the horses.

"What do you mean, 'for a while'?" Gabriel spied an old flour sack under the seat and used it to wipe down the horses.

"I hear they're sendin' a lot of troops back east. Some of the southern boys have already gone home." Mr. Lovelock rubbed the horses' ears and readjusted the harnesses.

Gabriel stopped wiping the horse and glanced across at Mr. Lovelock's narrow eyes and pointed nose. "Do you think they're goin' to fight a war?"

Mr. Lovelock pulled his hat off and wiped his forehead on his shirtsleeve. "I reckon they are if Mr. Lincoln gets elected. We'll know that by tomorrow. If it's going to happen, I can't think of a better man to be there than Mr. Lincoln. I met him a few times in Illinois. He came over to East Alton to campaign a time or two. But even a good man can't stop a war if men want to fight. By your drawl, I'm guessin' you're a southerner."

A slight breeze whipped up from the west. Gabriel fanned his untucked buckskin shirt. "I'm from Missouri, Mr. Lovelock. But I been on my own so long, I don't know what I am. I suppose I just sort of like folks to settle things peaceful."

Mr. Lovelock loaded the basket and water into the back of the wagon. "I'll drive on up the hill, son. The trail is kind of dangerous up ahead."

"Yes, sir." Gabriel climbed into the wagon.

They lurched forward on a road that looked little better than parallel game trails. "War is a horrible thing. I was in Mexico with General Scott."

"That's what Polk told me. In fact, Mama Lovelock said you wanted to name your daughter Scott."

Mr. Lovelock laughed and slapped his knee. "That isn't entirely true. I wanted to name her Scotina, but I reckon that's as bad, or worse. Anyway, we ought to avoid war whenever we can. And if it can't be avoided, do it with all your heart and skill. Half-hearted soldiers are the ones that die first."

"I don't know if I could be a soldier. I've spent my life tryin' to run away from fights."

"There's nothing wrong with that, Gabe. But every once in a while, you're going to have to make a stand for what is right, no matter what the cost. Slavery is no good, son. It's got to be stopped. It's wrong. I was just praying for some way to change it without anyone gettin' killed. I was hopin' it would get phased out gradual."

The road got steeper and narrower as it clung to the side of the mountain. "This is quite a drop down this canyon," Gabriel observed.

"You ought to see it when it's covered with snow and ice."

Gabriel's chin dropped, and his eyes widened. "You come up here in the snow and ice?"

Mr. Lovelock laughed. "No. I was teasing. The road is snowed shut from late November until March. You come from a Republican or Democrat family? Not that it matters to me, mind ya."

"I really don't know. I lost my kin before they schooled me much. I don't know much about politics, Mr. Lovelock. Most of my days is spent finding another meal." The grade grew steeper. Gabriel locked his knees on the wagon seat and hung onto the iron rail.

"You can't get away from politics, no matter where you go. Here we are at a Pony Express station in the Great Basin of Nevada. It's fifteen miles in either direction to the nearest neighbor. It takes us two days to get to the nearest town. We're isolated, and some weeks go by, and the only ones we've seen are the pony-riders themselves. Yet that station at Humboldt Flats is a political statement. It actually involves the struggle between the North and the South. Hang on, son. It gets narrow from here on up."

"Narrow? This wheel is hangin' over the edge as it is."

"You don't say?" Mr. Lovelock jerked the wagon to the left. "There. Is that better?"

"Ever' inch helps. How do you figure the station is a political statement?"

"For years old Butterfield has had the mail contract running through the southern route. Shoot, it goes clean into Texas and across the desert. It's a slow, roundabout way to get there. Takes forever. But the southern senators insist that's where the mail contract should go. They claim this central route through South Pass, Wyoming, is unusable in winter. The Pony Express was set up to prove the southerners wrong. It's a year-round trail, although them Sierra Nevadas can be bad in a blizzard. Russell, Majors, and Waddell are hoping to snag that mail contract."

"So the Pony Express is about the North and South?"

"Everything is politics, son."

"Mr. Lovelock, what happens if we meet a rig comin' down this trail?"

"You know, I've often wondered that myself. Are you scared?"

"No, sir . . . well, maybe just a little bit."

"Polk hides under a tarp in the back on this part of the trip. But you can see a hundred miles from up here. You see that mountain out by itself?"

Gabriel bit his lip and turned his head slowly to the south. "Eh, yep."

"That's Chocolate Butte."

"It don't look like chocolate."

"I reckon it did to someone sometime."

"Mr. Lovelock, if there's a war, are you goin' back to fight?"

"I figure I'm too old, but the boys will want to join."

"Where are your sons, Mr. Lovelock? If you don't mind me askin'."

"Will is in California. He's workin' for some surveyors who are surveying the entire state. He figures they're poking around for a train route across the Sierras, but no one will talk about it. Byron is runnin' freight up to Montana, and Keats is going to college in Ohio."

"You've got them scattered all over."

He roared. "It's a cinch they don't want to move to Humboldt Flats. Besides, we won't be here forever."

"Where will you go?"

"California, but I pledged to see this through. So I'll stay until they go completely broke. Ain't too many times a man gets to be a part of history twice in his life. I rode behind General Scott into Mexico City, and I've done my part to keep the pony-boys ridin'. I figure both events will make the history books."

"I don't reckon I've ever been a part of something historic."

"You can if you want to."

"You mean, I can join the Pony Express?"

"I was thinking of something more historic than that."

"What?"

"What do you figure is the most historic event that ever happened on this planet?"

"Shoot, I don't know, Mr. Lovelock."

"I'd say it was Jesus dying on the cross and that empty tomb three days later. You and me can be a part of that, you know."

"Is that the wood camp up there? Are those pine trees?"

"Son, I see you're avoidin' the subject."

"Yes, sir, I am."

"You can't run forever."

"Look, there's some others up here!"

"Okay, son, I'll quit preachin' at you."

Another wagon was nearly loaded. Two horses were tied to the back as four men split log rounds.

"Trent, you got yourself a helper now?" one of the men shouted as they approached.

"Yep. He's a good lad. Gabe, this is the Wheeler brothers, Whitey and Blackie. I imagine you can tell which is which. And this handsome Irishman is Marcus O'Daungty. This white-haired old man is L. I. Stubblefield."

"I'm younger than you, Lovelock," Stubblefield shot back.

"But that don't make you young, L. I." He turned to Gabriel. "They got swing stations east of here."

O'Daungty hiked over to the wagon. "You goin' back down tonight, Trent?"

"Yep. Just a quick load."

"You didn't leave the missus and Polk down at the station, did ya?" Whitey Wheeler asked.

Mr. Lovelock climbed down off the wagon. "Of course I did. What are you tryin' to say?"

Blackie ambled over, a splitting maul slung across his shoulder. "Didn't Johnny Rafter come through and warn ya?"

"Johnny hasn't been by in two weeks. Warn me about what?"

"About Paiutes, that's what," O'Daungty blurted out.

"What about 'em?" Gabriel questioned.

"There's a whole band of them on the warpath. They're comin' right down the Humboldt out of Idaho," Stubblefield reported.

"The Paiutes up north always get along with us," Mr. Lovelock replied. "It's that Pyramid Lake bunch that stirs things up."

"Johnny seen 'em comin'," Whitey declared. "Why do you think we're up here?"

"You plan on avoidin' the Indians?"

Blackie spat a wad of tobacco into the dirt and kicked dirt over it with his boot. "At least for the night we will."

"You want this load of wood?" Stubblefield offered. "We'll let you have it. That'll give us an excuse for stayin' up here."

Lovelock surveyed the wood camp. "Son, you unhook the team and water them over at that granite tank. We'll toss this wood into our wagon."

By the time Gabriel finished with the horses and got them hitched again, the five men had transferred the firewood.

"Good luck, Trent," O'Daungty said. "You got a gun, don't ya?"

"I got a shotgun with two shots. I reckon that will have to do. We'll be all right, boys. The Lord will deliver us."

"You got more faith than me," Stubblefield admitted.

They didn't say anything to each other as they pulled out of the wood camp. Mr. Lovelock yanked back on the lead line and forced the team to creep down the mountain.

And he whistled.

"Do you think Indians are really comin', Mr. Lovelock?" Gabriel asked.

All the features on Mr. Lovelock's face looked frozen and emotionless. "I reckon there's some truth to it."

"Do you think the station at Humboldt Flats will be in danger?"

"If they come down the Humboldt River."

Gabriel's side of the wagon was tucked up against the mountainside now. "How come we aren't goin' faster then?"

"'Cause we'll plunge over the edge and both be killed. Can't help Mama and Polk that way, could we?"

"No, sir, I don't reckon we could. What're we goin' to do?"

"Get back as fast as we can without wreckin' and pray a lot."

"They will be okay, won't they? Polk and Mama Lovelock will be okay?" Gabriel could hear his voice break.

"Why don't you pray for us, son," Mr. Lovelock suggested. "With that sun in our eyes, I need to keep on top of this trail."

"I ain't never prayed," Gabriel blurted out.

"Never? Everyone prays. In the war even heathen nonbelievers prayed when they got scared enough."

"I ain't never prayed out loud."

"Go ahead. Just talk to God like He was sittin' here with us."

Gabriel's tongue was so dry it stuck to the roof of his mouth. "God, this is me, and I'm scared for Mama Lovelock and Polk. You don't have to give me nothin' 'cause I don't deserve it. But them two is sweet and true, and if You don't protect the likes of them, I don't reckon anyone in this world has got a chance. So now it's up to You to do Your part, and we'll do ours . . . eh . . ."

"In Jesus' name, amen," Mr. Lovelock added. "You did fine. You spoke with your heart, and that's what a man's got to do."

"I'm scared to death, Mr. Lovelock."

"You scared of Paiutes, or you scared of talking to God?"

"Both," Gabriel admitted.

Two men on horseback and leading pack mules waited for them at the base of the mountains where the road hit the desert. Mr. Lovelock pulled up the wagon. "I'm in a hurry, boys. Is there anything I can do for you?"

"Is this the trail up to the diggin's at Chocolate Butte?"

"Nope. Just a wood camp up here. Chocolate Butte is ten miles south. But there's no prospectin' there."

"It's new," reported the gray-headed man with a full beard. "Not many know about it."

Gabriel studied the middle-aged man. "Mr. Davis, is that you?"

The man rode closer to the wagon and squinted his eyes. "Gabe? You've grown up, son. I didn't recognize you."

Mr. Lovelock glanced at Gabriel. "You two know each other?"

"I tended his camp a couple years ago in Colorado. Everett Davis, this is Mr. Trent Lovelock. There really isn't any gold at Chocolate Butte. I heard how that story got started, and it's a more fanciful rumor than the one about Pike's Peak."

Davis rubbed his scraggly beard. "I still say there's gold up behind Pike's Peak. Someday someone will find it. Ten miles south, you say?"

"Yes, but there's nothin' down there," Lovelock repeated.

"I reckon we'll check it out. As long as we're this close, we'll take a look. There's always a little truth behind ever' rumor. It's a cinch we ain't goin' back to the river."

"Why's that?" Gabriel asked.

"There's a party of Paiutes comin'."

"How many?" Lovelock asked.

"Can't tell from a distance. Most of them are on foot. You know how them Paiutes are. They travel in swarms. I wouldn't go out there if I was you," Davis warned.

"Yes, you would," Trent Lovelock said as he slapped the lead lines. "I've got a wife and daughter out there."

SEVEN

The Great Basin still looked empty. Like their trip across earlier, there were no people, no animals, no buildings, no houses, no movement.

But everything felt different.

"They're goin' to be all right. I just know they'll be all right!" Gabriel muttered.

Mr. Lovelock squinted his eyes against the declining sun. The creases on his face were frozen with worry. He glared at the western horizon without glancing at Gabriel. "That's right, son. They will be fine. You prayed, and we'll have to trust the Lord."

For several minutes the only sound was the creaking of the loaded wagon and Mr. Lovelock's whistling.

"I ain't too good at prayin'," Gabriel blurted out. "Maybe you ought to pray too."

"I did. Didn't you hear me amen your prayer? When I said 'amen,' that meant I was agreeing with you. It became my prayer too. So there was two prayers said."

"But what . . . what if I did it wrong?"

"You can't do prayer wrong if you talk from your heart. The Lord always listens to heart talk. Now head talk . . . When we try to impress Him with words, I reckon it can bore Him to tears. It bores me when someone just throws a bunch of words out without conviction. Course, we can just keep on prayin'."

"Out loud?"

"No, just in our hearts."

The trail was rutted and bumpy, and the loaded wagon seemed to magnify every bang, rattle, and axle squeak. Gabriel held onto the iron wagon rail.

Now, God, it ain't right that two fine people like Polk and Mama Lovelock have their futures dependent on the prayers of a no-account like me. I want to do somethin' to help them. I'll do whatever, even if it kills me. I mean it, Lord. You know I mean it 'cause Mr. Lovelock said You listen to hearts.

"Not all Indians are bloodthirsty, are they?" Gabriel asked.

Mr. Lovelock stopped whistling. "No. Some are nice. Some are mean. And a whole lot of them are scared. Not too much different than us."

"There were some at Ft. Bridger that were nice to me. They were havin' a weddin'. This Indian man's daughter was marryin' one of the clerks at the fort. She wore a purple weddin' dress. I ain't never heard of a purple weddin' dress, but her daddy said she always wore purple. Her name was Virginia, just like Mama Lovelock's. That wasn't her Indian name. Her Indian name was Shy Bear. She surely wasn't shy that day. Anyway, her daddy, who was called Two Bears, gave me a whole pouch full of buffalo jerky. It lasted me nearly two weeks. Not all Indians are mean. I guess I'm talkin' too much, but that's 'cause I'm nervous."

"It's okay, son. I whistle when I'm nervous. You can talk all you want."

Mr. Lovelock started to whistle "Amazing Grace."

Gabriel let out a long, slow sigh and bit his lip.

I really would give my life for them, God. It would make my life successful. Savin' Mama Lovelock and Polk, why, that would make fourteen miserable years worthwhile. It gives purpose to being in this world. It gives me a reason for wanderin' out here in the desert. It's like a destiny. I ain't never had a destiny. None that I know'd of anyways.

"Do you know any nice Paiutes?" Gabriel blurted out.

Mr. Lovelock slapped the leather lead lines to push the team faster. Then he stopped whistling and wiped his mustache. "We have visitors from time to time. We try to treat them with kindness and not suspicion. Usually they just want some fresh water. For a long time, that spring at Humboldt Flats was their watering hole."

"You said suspicion. You suspect they might try to scalp you?"

"Not so much that, but they will try to steal. It's a way of life for them. I don't even know if they figure it's wrong."

"There are some white boys on the streets of St. Joseph that don't act much different than that."

"That's true, son. We all have to face judgment one day, no matter what color we are."

"Yes, sir, I reckon we will." Gabriel's voice trailed off into the squeak of the axles.

Mr. Lovelock whistled again. This time Gabriel didn't recognize the tune.

I've known the Lovelocks just twenty-four hours, and I'm ready to die for them. I don't know what makes that so. I don't know how come anyone is willin' to die for anyone else. But I know it's true. Maybe You put it in my heart, with Mr. Lovelock talkin' about Jesus dyin' for us and all. Anyway, I'm glad I can say it and mean it in my heart.

Gabriel glanced back at the wagonload of firewood. "Mr. Lovelock, maybe we shouldn't have brought a load of wood. We could have raced these horses back if it was empty."

"Me and the Lord have been discussing that very matter."

"I thought you were whistlin'."

"I can drive a team, whistle, fret, and talk to the Lord all at the same time. Isn't that somethin'?"

"What did you and Him decide? I could climb back there and start tossin' out wood to lighten the load. We could always come back and scoop it up."

"I thought of that too, but the Lord chastised me."

"How did He do that?"

"He said, 'Lovelock, do you trust Me with an empty wagon but not with a loaded wagon?'"

"What did you tell Him?"

"I pondered it for a while. And I realized that once the wagon was empty, I'd probably keep on frettin'. And I'd want to toss off the tailgate and the side rails, and pretty soon I'd cut the teams loose, and we'd ride them bareback."

"You think we should?"

"Nope. 'Cause then I'd just prove that I wasn't trusting Him at all. So I just up and decided that we need this full load of wood to prove that we're trusting Him."

"So we're goin' to leave the wood?"

"All the way to the station." When Mr. Lovelock whistled another tune, the horses laid their ears back and raced faster.

If we get through this, Lord, I'll ask Polk or Mama Lovelock to teach me how to pray right. I'm a quick learner, Lord. You know that, I reckon.

When they hit a hole, Gabriel bounced a foot off the seat. He felt Mr. Lovelock grab his shoulder and shove him back down.

Maybe not Polk. She might laugh. I'll ask Mama Lovelock. She don't laugh. She just hugs me and cries.

Out of the corner of his eye, Gabe spotted several sticks of firewood bounce out of the wagon, but they didn't slow down at all.

That was the best hug I ever got in my life. A boy surely could get used to hugs like that. Lord, let me live long enough to get one more of Mama Lovelock's hugs.

For the first time since they hit the desert floor, Mr. Lovelock turned his head and glanced at Gabriel. "Are you prayin', son?"

"Yes, sir. I am."

"I thought you said you didn't pray much."

"I changed my mind."

"That's good. That's real good. You won't regret it. No, son, you won't regret it."

The wind drifted into their faces and kept the dust from the wagon wheels behind them. The air cooled as they rumbled west, and the buckskin shirt felt good on Gabriel's arms and shoulders. "Is it gettin' colder?" he asked. "Or am I just gettin' nervous goose bumps?"

"Some of both. I think we lost our warm weather. Feels like a cold Oregon wind blowing down. I expect ice on the water trough tonight. Kind of a late summer we've been enjoying."

"I don't reckon we ought to be talkin' about the weather."

"We're doing what we need to be doing. We're going home as fast as faith and two Pony Express horses will pull us. No matter what we talk about, it won't change that."

Mr. Lovelock whistled.

Gabriel pondered.

And neither talked for a long time.

"I see the trees!" Gabriel cried.

"Are you sure?"

"Yes, sir. I got good eyes. There ain't any other trees out here, are there?"

"Nope, that must be them. Don't reckon you can see anything else?"

"No, sir, just trees. We're still a couple of miles away, I think."

"There's the trees, all right. And if the building was on fire, we'd see it burning from here."

"Burnin'? Is that what they'd do?"

"It happened over by Pyramid Lake. They burned down three swing stations."

"Humboldt Flats ain't burnin'."

They rumbled west for several more minutes.

"Can you see anything else?"

"I can see the station house. And corrals."

"Everything's kind of blurry for me at this distance."

The wagon rattled.

Hooves pounded.

Axles squeaked.

Gabriel's heart thumped.

"There's horses out front," Gabriel shouted.

"Horses?"

"Horses and dogs and stuff."

"Stuff? What do you mean, stuff?"

"I don't know. Packs or piles or bales or . . . stuff."

"Then they're there."

"The Paiutes?"

"Yep. They're at the station."

"It's really the Indians?"

"Yep. Here, you take the ribbons and scoot over and drive."

Gabriel grabbed the worn leather lead lines and scooted across the wooden wagon seat while Mr. Lovelock crawled around to the other side. "What're you goin' to do?"

"Grab my scatter gun." Mr. Lovelock pulled a pocket pistol out of his boot.

"I thought you only had the shotgun."

"That's all I mentioned at the wood camp. No man in this wild country needs to reveal what he's totin', not until it's time."

Gabriel reached down and pulled his knife from his boot.

Mr. Lovelock nodded his head.

"I don't see anyone at the station. Maybe they're around back," Gabriel suggested.

"Or in the house," Mr. Lovelock added.

Gabriel held the knife with one hand and the lead lines with the other. "What're we goin' to do if there's a fight?"

"We're going to fight to win, son."

"Do you want me to drive up to the front door?"

"Circle to the north and drive it straight between the backdoor and barn. Are you scared?"

"Yes, sir, I am."

"Good. I'm glad I'm not the only one."

"You're scared? But you have faith. You're trustin' the Lord."

"Yeah, but I'm not perfect. Right about now my faith is waning a bit. But God is faithful even when we waver. Come on, whip that team on. It's time to meet our fate."

Gabriel gripped his knife handle in his teeth and the lead lines in both hands. The horses thundered across the open wilderness as he circled the station.

"They're all by the back door," Mr. Lovelock shouted.

Gabriel spotted a dozen partially clothed, dark-skinned people of various sizes huddled together. *They've got the women surrounded. Oh, no . . . no . . . no, Lord. Please!*

"Slow it down, son. Slow it down."

The Indians turned to watch them approach, but didn't make a move toward them. Polk broke free from the huddle and raced to the wagon.

"Daddy! Gabriel!" she shouted. "I can't believe you got back so soon. That was the fastest load of wood you ever fetched."

"Are you okay, darlin'?" Mr. Lovelock asked as he jumped off the wagon.

"Oh, yes, isn't it exciting? We have some Paiute visitors. Why does Gabe have that knife in his mouth?"

"He was, eh, just showing me how he would ride

into a camp of hostile Indians. You take care of the ponies, son. We'll unload the firewood later."

Gabriel slipped his knife back into the sheath in his boot and climbed off the wagon.

"You ran the horses too fast," she said. "You should take it easy with a heavy load."

"We thought there might be trouble. We couldn't tell from a distance."

"Did you come roaring in here to save me?" Polk asked.

Gabriel glanced down at his boots. "You and Mama Lovelock. I didn't know they was friendly."

Polk threw her arms around Gabriel and hugged him tight.

He pulled back. "What did you do that for? I didn't do anything."

"I hugged you for what you thought you were doing, Gabriel Young."

He grabbed the old flour sack under the wagon seat and began to rub down the horses. "What's goin' on here, Polk?"

"They're all one big family. A man is moving his mother, grandmother, a lame brother, sister-in-law, and several nieces and nephews down to Walker Lake. They used to live up on the Oregon border, but there's trouble up there, and he wanted to move them out of danger."

"How do you know?"

"The man can speak English. They asked for some fresh water, but you know Mama. She insisted on feeding them. You see the little girl in the yellow dress? That's one of my old dresses. She showed up buck naked, and Mama gave her a dress."

Gabriel pulled the harness and rigging off the team. "How do you feed that many?"

"Mama made them fry cakes. They just roll them up and dip them in a bowl of molasses she has on the back step. That's why they're huddled around there. They're waiting their turn for another fry cake."

Gabriel heard Mr. Lovelock's deep laugh and spied him on the back step next to his wife.

"This is an answer to prayer, Polk."

"Did you pray for me, Gabriel? I didn't think you believed in prayer."

"I do now. I reckon I learned a lot of things today."

"Did my daddy whistle while he was driving back to the station?"

"Yes, he did. Real loud."

"He was worried then."

"But he said we could trust the Lord. I reckon he was right." Gabriel led the team of horses toward the water trough just as a barefoot Indian wearing buckskin trousers and a wool shirt broke away from the others and headed that way too.

"That's the one who speaks English. I'll introduce you."

"I don't reckon I have anything to visit with him about."

"You aren't afraid, are you?"

"Of course not."

"Then why are you sweating so much?"

"That's 'cause—'cause . . . you hugged me."

Polk clapped her hands. "That's a wonderful lie, Gabriel Young. I think I'll choose to believe it. How old do you think he is?"

"I don't know. About twenty or so, I guess. I can't ever tell Indian ages."

"He doesn't know either. I asked him how old he was, and he said he was born before it mattered. Isn't that funny? They don't even count the years."

"When you think about it, I don't reckon it does matter."

The Indian walked up to them as they led the horses to the water.

"Your ponies are tired," he remarked.

"They pulled a heavy load," Gabriel murmured.

The Indian looked at Polk. "Is he your husband?"

"Husband?" Gabriel gulped. "We ain't married. I'm only fourteen years old."

The Indian smiled. "In that case, perhaps I should marry her."

Gabriel's mouth dropped open.

"But she is too sickly white. It's not healthy to be that pale. I do not need another sickly relative," he laughed.

"He teases a lot," Polk grinned. She grabbed Gabriel's arm. "This is my friend Gabriel Young."

"Gabriel? Were you named after the angel?"

"I suppose," Gabriel murmured.

Then she grabbed the Indian's arm. "And this is my new friend Fergus."

"I was named after a cow," the Indian joked.

"A cow?" Gabriel said.

"My mother's favorite cow." He grinned.

"Are you goin' to camp here tonight?" Polk asked.

"No, we have a campsite out in the lava rocks west of here. It is a small cave and very comfortable. It will be out of the storm."

Gabriel studied the pale blue twilight sky. "Storm? There aren't any clouds in the sky."

Fergus nodded at a white-haired woman with bent shoulders and a leather-tough, wrinkled face that almost hid her eyes. "Grandmother says it will storm tonight."

"Is she ever wrong?" Polk asked.

Fergus scooped water from the trough and drank out of his hand. "Not yet. But she is still young." His wide smile revealed straight white teeth.

EIGHT

Molasses ran out.

Paiutes left.

Horses were put away.

Firewood stacked.

Supper cooked.

Polk sat at the side of the table that faced the rear wall of the big room that served as kitchen, dining room, living room, and station office. Mr. Lovelock stood behind a chair near the fireplace. Mrs. Lovelock filled plates from pots on a woodstove tucked in the corner.

Gabriel lingered near the back door.

"Gabe, your chair is here across from Polk." Mr. Lovelock pointed.

"It don't seem right for me to be bargin' in on you folks."

"I'm going to take that as a personal insult that you don't like us," Mrs. Lovelock declared. "Now, that's your chair . . . tonight . . . tomorrow . . . and every day that you're with us. You understand?"

"Yes, Mama Lovelock."

She brushed an errant strand of gray-streaked brown hair out of her eyes. "Now, that's better."

He plodded over and plopped down in the chair across from Polk.

"Hehhh-hem!" Polk cleared her throat.

Gabriel looked around. "Did I do somethin' wrong already?" He shot to his feet. "Where did you want me to sit?"

"It's customary for the men to remain standing until all the ladies are seated," Mr. Lovelock explained.

"It is? You see, I don't even know the rules."

Mrs. Lovelock brought a huge green pottery bowl over to the table. She gave Gabriel a quick hug. "That's quite all right, honey. I'm sure Sissy will school you."

"Oh, yes!" Polk replied.

They devoured brown gravy stew with chunks of beef, potatoes, and turnips, sopped up with thick sourdough bread covered with pale butter, topped off with cactus jelly.

Mrs. Lovelock served coffee and black bread pudding for dessert.

All four drank coffee.

"The pudding is a little flat," she remarked. "I seem to have run out of molasses faster than I anticipated."

"That company beef has been tough," Mr. Lovelock added. "I'm going to mention that to the superintendent next time he comes through."

"I baked the bread," Polk said. "It's not as good as Mama's."

Gabriel shook his head. "I can tell you it's one of the nicest meals I've had in a long time. When you have to hunt for food, I reckon you appreciate it more."

"You're absolutely right, my Gabe," Mrs. Lovelock said. "We complain way too much."

"No, I didn't mean it that way. It's just . . . I ain't . . . Well, I ain't sat down at a table and had a meal in months. And then it's in a cafe or . . . or . . ."

"Never mind the past," Mrs. Lovelock interrupted. "This is your table now."

"You'll have to teach me the rules."

"You're doin' very good, honey," Mrs. Lovelock insisted. "Unlike some, you don't have your elbows on the table."

Polk sat straight up and pulled her elbows back.

"But you might enjoy using a fork and spoon when you eat stew, although you did quite well with just a knife and a hunk of bread."

Gabriel stared at the silverware. "I'll remember next time, Mama Lovelock. I'm a quick learner."

After the table was cleared, all four continued to sit at the table and sip coffee.

"Gabe, Polk told us that you lost your folks in a train wreck and were raised by grandparents. Do you have any other kin around, son?" Mr. Lovelock asked.

"I don't know. My mama was an only child, and it was her parents that I lived with. They didn't like my daddy's kin. I mean, it was kind of like a feud, you might say. So they never told me about them at all."

"Did your grandparents die at the same time?" Mrs. Lovelock asked.

"No, about six months apart. There was a lot of cholera goin' around that winter. I reckon they were too old to fight it off."

"How old were they?" Polk asked.

"Grandma was fifty-four. Grandpa was fifty-two, but he died first."

"What happened then?" Mrs. Lovelock prodded.

"I ran and got the doctor when Grandma didn't wake up. The doc and his wife hurried back and shooed me to the next room. But I listened to them at the door. They started talkin' about the children's asylum. That's when I decided to grab my coat and leave."

"You just left?" Polk asked.

"I didn't want to live in some orphanage."

"How old were you, honey?" Mrs. Lovelock asked.

"Nine."

"Nine years old and you left home?" Mrs. Lovelock gasped.

"I was almost ten," he amended.

"Oh dear . . . oh dear." Mrs. Lovelock scurried to the backroom.

"I didn't hurt her feelin's, did I?" Gabriel asked.

"No, son. Mama just gets teary when she thinks of children goin' through rough times. She's always been that way. Always will. Well, we got a big day tomorrow, and I'm countin' on your help."

"I'll do whatever I can. What's the big day?"

"Tomorrow's rider from the east is supposed to bring the news of who won the election."

"I didn't know it was that important."

"They voted four days ago. Now it's time to get the result. The pony-rider tomorrow will be in a greater hurry than normal."

"They sent us a $400 horse for him to ride. They're trying to set a record for how fast they can ride the mail west," Polk informed him.

"Not only that, but they want to keep all that gold in California in the right hands. They want that election news to get west in a hurry," Mr. Lovelock explained.

"What are you going to do different?" Gabriel asked.

"I built a raised boardwalk so he doesn't have to get to the ground to change horses."

"And I made a cotton lunch bag that slips over the saddle horn as soon as he tosses the mochila on it," Polk said. "On one side of the sack is beef and bread. On the other side, oats for his horse."

"I ain't never seen anyone grain a horse while it was gallopin'."

"You can just lean forward and shove some in the horse's mouth," Polk explained. "At least, I think you can."

"What do you want me to do?"

"You catch the off horse and get him out of the way as quick as you can. We'll practice a little in the morning. We'll be making history," Mr. Lovelock said.

"Really?"

"It's an important election, son. Maybe the most important since Washington took the reins. Here we are stuck in the middle of the Nevada high desert, and yet we play a part in history."

"Daddy is always dramatic when it comes to politics," Polk said.

"I'm lookin' forward to chores. Then I'll feel like I'm earnin' my keep."

Mrs. Lovelock emerged from the backroom with a linen handkerchief. "Honey, a nine-year-old should never have to earn his keep."

"But I'm fourteen now."

"You have some chores saved up."

"Robert Chester Michaels is ridin' this route tomorrow. He's the fastest of the pony-riders in this area," Polk reported.

"You folks are gettin' me excited."

"We've been sort of planning it for weeks. I'm goin' to hang red, white, and blue ribbons all along the corral tomorrow," Polk announced.

"And even though no one will see us, we'll all wear our best clothes," Mrs. Lovelock said.

"These are the only clothes I have," Gabriel reminded them.

"Then they are your best. That shirt looks nice on you," Mrs. Lovelock complimented him. "Don't you think so, Sissy?"

"Oh, yes, and it covers your skinny ribs."

"Polk Lovelock!"

"Well, it does."

"I reckon they won't be skinny long, the way you folks is stuffin' me."

"I'm going to be giving Mr. Lovelock a haircut tomorrow morning to commemorate the event. Would you like one too, Gabe?" Mrs. Lovelock asked.

"That's okay, ma'am. I don't reckon I need one."

Polk nodded her head up and down.

"Maybe I do need just a trim," he said.

"It hangs down to your shoulders," Polk murmured.

"I ain't had time or money to cut it in a while."

"Where did you get it cut last?"

"A lady—well, a woman in Colorado cut it for me about a year ago, I reckon."

"Gabe and me will go check the corrals," Mr. Lovelock said. "Then we should all get to bed."

"This has been purtnear the most exciting day of my life. I'm ready to stretch out on that soft hay in the barn," Gabriel sighed.

"You'll do no such thing," Mrs. Lovelock snapped. "You're sleeping on that couch by the front door. That's your bed in this house, and I won't tolerate one word of protest from you."

Gabriel just stared at the woman.

"Mama can get a little testy if you don't see things her way," Mr. Lovelock laughed.

Gabriel swallowed hard. "I ain't goin' to argue with Mama Lovelock."

"You see, Daddy," Polk squealed, "he does learn fast."

When he and Mr. Lovelock came back inside, Gabe spied a pillow in a cotton case and two gray wool blankets stacked on the leather couch. He pulled off his boots and neatly folded his socks. He wiggled his toes in the lantern light and could hear voices and laughter in the room that served as a bedroom for the Lovelocks.

Gabriel Young, you struck gold here. This is better than gold. This is a real family, and they took you in. Course, they can put you out again, but there's no reason to dwell on that. Last night I was livin' in a hole in the ground, and tonight I'm in a castle.

He pulled off the buckskin shirt, folded it, and stacked it by the socks. Then he sat back on the couch, leaned his head against the cushion, and closed his eyes.

That Indian said they were stayin' in a cave in the lava rocks. It can't be that same cave. It wasn't hardly big enough for two. Maybe three people if you scrunched in tight.

"Daddy wants to know if you want to borrow one of his night shirts?" a soft voice said.

Gabriel blinked his eyes open. He yanked a gray wool blanket across his bare chest. "No!" he blurted out.

Polk stood in front of him, wearing a long flannel gown buttoned high at the neck. Her hands didn't come out of the sleeves. "This is my mama's gown. I've got mine on under this one."

Gabriel continued to clutch the wool blanket to his chest. "That's cozy. But I don't reckon I need a night shirt. I never had one."

"Come winter, you'll want one."

"Maybe so, but . . . not now."

"You haven't been around girls much, have you?"

"Not ones my age."

She shoved a small, fat book at him. "Mama said this is a present for you."

"What is it?"

"It's a Bible. Do you have one?"

"I ain't never had one, but I can't take it."

"I was hopin' you'd say that."

"Why?"

"'Cause Mama said if you put up a protest, I could clobber you with it."

Gabriel plucked the Bible from her hands. "I just can't keep takin' gifts. It ain't right."

"This is a company Bible. We got plenty of them. Mr. Majors gives one free to every pony-rider. And we have extras. Daddy said you're helping tend a Pony Express station, and that qualifies you for one. You earned it hauling the wood down and tending horses."

"I do know how to read. Grandma taught me. But them big words is tough."

"I have trouble with some of them too, but my mama and daddy know every big word in the Bible. Ask them if you need help. Mama said maybe you and me ought to start a school."

"What do you mean, start a school?"

"She'd be the teacher, and we'd be the pupils. She's been teaching me since we moved to Humboldt Flats last spring, just an hour or two a day."

"I'd like that, but I don't want to shirk my chores."

"Daddy said you'd say that. He said to tell you he only has about four hours of chores a day, and the rest of the time is yours."

"I hardly earn my meals in four hours."

"Gabriel Young, you're absolutely the most stubborn, impossible boy I ever met," she huffed.

He studied her for a minute.

"What're you staring at?" she asked.

"Did you know your ears and nose wiggle at the same time when you get mad?"

"They do not," she protested.

"Yes, they do. And it looks cute," he added.

A wide smile beamed across her face. Her light green eyes shone in the lantern light. "In that case . . . goodnight, Gabriel Young."

"Goodnight, Polk Lovelock."

He watched her walk across the room and close the door.

Did I just call her cute? I ain't never called any girl cute in my life.

Gabriel made up his bed and stretched out on the

couch, leaving the oil lantern burning. He pulled the clean wool blankets up to his chin and left his arms out, holding the small, thick Bible.

He turned the thin pages and began to read. He was still reading when Mrs. Lovelock scooted into the room.

"Excuse me, honey. I saw the light on and knew you weren't sleeping. I need to get my jar of menthol salve."

"I was readin'."

"I'm glad to see that."

"I remember some of the stories that Grandma used to tell me."

She plucked up a small green glass jar from the counter. "What part are you reading?"

He stared at the book. "It's called the Preface to King James."

She smiled. "The preface? No, that's not even the Scriptures. That's just what the Bible translators told the king of England. Why don't you read in the book of Mark?"

"Okay, what page is that on?"

She took the Bible from his hand and thumbed through toward the back. "Here. You can start right there."

"What should I be looking for? Will it tell me what sins I ought to stop doin'?"

"Yes, it might. But I think you probably already know those, don't you?"

"I reckon so."

"Why don't you study to see what it tells you about Jesus? Save up those thoughts in your mind. Sooner or later you'll have to decide if you believe them or not."

"I like that. No one ever explained it to me before."

"Had your mama lived, I'm sure she would have told you the same thing."

Gabriel stared across the room at the darkened table. "You know I can't even remember my mama."

She reached over and patted his head. "Don't you have any portraits of them at all?"

"No. But I do remember my grandma. I remember her not wakin' up that mornin', and she was cold and stiff. But she did look peaceful."

Mrs. Lovelock continued to pat his head as she wiped her eyes on her sleeve. "You read a little while, and then turn out the lantern and get some sleep. We do have an exciting day tomorrow."

"You folks are surely bein' nice to me."

She smiled. "You're my special angel, young man."

"What do you mean?"

"My heart was melancholy, and the Lord sent me my very own Gabriel. Goodnight, my Gabe."

"Goodnight, Mama Lovelock."

NINE

The moment he heard a boot heel on the swept wooden floor, Gabriel leaped from the couch. "Is that you, Mr. Lovelock?"

"Sorry to wake you, son. You hear that thunder?"

"Yes, sir."

"That old Indian grandma was right about a storm. It's a little early, but the horses are actin' up. I'm goin' to go check on them."

"I'll go with you."

"No need for that, son."

"I'd feel much better about myself if you let me."

There was silence in the pitch-dark room, then a flicker of a sulfur match. "I'll build up a fire in the stove while you get ready," Mr. Lovelock said.

Gabriel dressed and jammed on his boots and his old slouch hat.

"It's blowing and raining out there, son. Let's run to the barn first off. You carry the lantern." Mr. Lovelock grabbed his shotgun and opened the back door.

Rain pelted their faces. The wind blew out the lantern.

"Do you hear the horses?" Mr. Lovelock shouted.

"They're about ready to bolt. Something stirred them up. We got to get them settled down."

They raced through the storm to the barn. Gabriel heard the horses' panicked whinnies. Inside the barn he still felt the wind blow, but it was dry. Mr. Lovelock grabbed his arm. "Let me see if I can get that lantern lit in here."

It took three attempts, but finally the lantern stayed lit, and Mr. Lovelock propped it up on a barrel. "Grab a handful of oats. Even in the rain maybe they can smell that. It might distract them from whatever spooked them."

Gabriel jammed both hands into the barrel of oats.

"It'll be dark out there; so you'll have to sing above the storm."

"Sing?"

"It's too wet to whistle. You got to talk to them or sing. They need to hear a human voice so they don't think somethin' scary is sneakin' up on them. I'll grab a flake of hay from the loft."

The horrible screech sounded like fingernails on a slate, only ten times louder. Every hair on Gabriel's head stood up. His knees quivered. His tongue felt like a log jammed down his throat. He couldn't move.

A large mountain lion lunged onto Mr. Lovelock's shoulder from the hay loft, drawing blood from his neck and arm.

"Get him off," Mr. Lovelock yelled. He spun around and tried to wrestle the cat to the floor.

Blood slapped against Gabe's face. He threw the grain at the mountain lion. The cat jerked his head away from Mr. Lovelock and snarled. Gabriel seized his knife out of his boot and took a wild slice at the animal with one motion.

A dark red ribbon of blood stained the animal's yellow-brown hair on its shoulder. The cat leaped to the dirt floor and limped out into the storm.

Blood flowed between Mr. Lovelock's fingers as he clamped his hand to his neck. "Stop the horses from breaking out, Gabe!" he shouted.

"You're bleedin'," Gabriel yelled back.

"The horses, son. Stand at the gate and shout back in. Sing 'em quiet. Hurry!"

Gabriel dashed out of the barn into the rain. The back door of the station swung open. A bolt of lightning revealed Mrs. Lovelock in her flannel gown. "What happened, my Gabe?" she hollered into the rain.

"Mr. Lovelock was attacked by a mountain lion. He's bleedin' awful bad, and I got to still the horses."

Barefoot, Mrs. Lovelock ran through the mud to the barn.

Gabriel sprinted to the corrals. "Settle down. . . . Settle down, boys," he shouted. "It'll be all right. . . . The cat's gone. Settle down."

He could hear them kick at the fence rails.

Sing them down, Gabriel. Sing them down.

Thunder growled. Lightning flashed. He could see the panic in their eyes. *They're goin' to run, and no fence in the world will hold them.*

Gabriel took a big, deep breath. Rain poured off his hat. His face was wet. His hands were cold. He couldn't keep his knees from shaking.

"'Amazing grace, how sweet the sound . . .'" It sounded more like a croaky shout than a song. "'. . . that saved a wretch like me. I once was lost, but now am found, was blind but now I see!'"

The horses shuffled, milled.

I don't know any other verses, Lord. Help me. Help Mr. Lovelock.

"'Amazing grace,'" he shouted again.

The lightning flashed.

"'How sweet the sound . . .'"

The thunder roared like a cannon on the Fourth of July.

"'. . . that saved . . .'"

The horses stampeded in circles in the corral.

"'. . . a wretch like me.'"

The rain blew sideways from the west.

"'I once was lost . . .'"

It stung his face.

"'. . . but now am found . . .'"

And soaked his britches.

"'Was blind . . .'"

He knew somewhere on his wet cheeks were tears.

"'. . . but now I see.'"

Over.

And over.

And over he shouted as he sprinted from one part of the corral to another.

The storm raged.

The rain hammered.

The lightning eased.

The thunder ceased.

Gabriel kept singing.

And singing.

And the horses stayed in the corrals.

He was cold, soaked to the bone, and hoarse when Polk scampered to his side. The sky had turned pre-dawn gray.

It had stopped raining and left a slimy coat of mud. She was wearing her father's heavy coat and hat.

"Daddy said the horses were calm enough, and you should come in the house before you catch your death of ague."

"How is he?"

"He's covered with iodine right now, but Mama says he'll do fine," she reported.

"He was bleedin' bad." Gabriel choked the words out in a rough whisper.

"Daddy bleeds a lot. He always says he has too much blood."

"He don't now," Gabriel declared.

Inside the house a fire roared in the fireplace. A shirtless Trent Lovelock sat on a kitchen chair. Mrs. Lovelock—gown hanging wet and splattered with mud, iodine, and blood—doctored his wounds.

"The horses settled down. None of them broke out," Polk reported.

Gabriel hiked over to the fire. "I'm sorry for trackin' in some mud, but I couldn't find a dry spot to wipe my feet."

"There's my hero," Mrs. Lovelock greeted him. "Sissy, get my Gabe a cup of coffee and stir him up some white gravy for those biscuits."

Gabriel eased down on the rock hearth and tugged off his wet boots. His feet felt raw and frozen. "I ain't no hero. I just sort of reacted without thinkin' about it."

Mr. Lovelock winced as a new wound was discovered by the sting of rubbing alcohol. "That's all any hero does, son. There's somethin' heroic deep inside that just kicks in during a time of panic."

"All I did is what ought to be done. Anyone else

would have done the same." Gabriel peeled off his wet socks and spread them out by the fire. "Are you goin' to be all right?"

Trent Lovelock flexed his broad, muscled shoulders. One was wrapped with linen. "I'll have some scars and scratches for a long time, but I can live with that, son. You saved my life."

"I don't know about that. You probably could have wrestled him off." The hot coffee warmed his fingers through the tin cup.

"Not without worse wounds. If he had ripped through an artery, I'd be dead by now. Not only that, but you saved the ponies. Mama, can you imagine what our lives would be like at this moment if the Lord hadn't sent Gabriel Young to us?"

Mrs. Lovelock stepped back and folded her arms. "I shudder to think of it, Daddy. I told him last night I thought he was my angel. Now I know it for sure. I must look horrible. Sissy, you take care of the men. I'm going to change. I'll just have to let you bleed awhile, Trent, and see what wounds I missed." She paused at the doorway to the bedroom. "And both of you still need a haircut."

Gabriel sipped on hot coffee, felt the heat of the fire, and watched the steam rise off his buckskin shirt. "I suppose it was the mountain lion that spooked the horses."

"Yep," Mr. Lovelock said. "The storm drove the animal into the barn. I scared it, and you reacted."

"Are you goin' to be able to get things ready for the pony-rider today?"

"You might have to help me more than I thought."

"I can do it."

"I have no doubt that you can, son."

Polk carried the coffeepot over to Gabriel. "Would you like a refill?"

"Thank ya, Polk, but you don't need to wait on me."

"Oh, yes, I do. Mama said I had to take care of the . . . men." When she said "men," both her ears and her nose wiggled.

Gabriel washed his hair in the sunlight next to the water trough by the corral and toweled it off. When he got into the house, Mr. Lovelock pulled on his shirt. "It's your turn for a haircut, son."

"You don't look much different," Gabriel commented.

"Look at all the hair on that sheet." Mrs. Lovelock pointed to the floor.

"I've seen dogs shed more than that in one sittin'," Gabriel replied. "Are you sure you didn't use him just to prime the pump?"

Mrs. Lovelock laughed.

"That boy's onto you, Mama," Mr. Lovelock said. "I'm going to check on those horses now."

Mrs. Lovelock laid the scissors down and stepped over to the counter. "I'm going to slice some onions. Sissy, see that my Gabe's hair gets combed out."

Polk stepped up behind him and tied a sheet around his neck.

"I can comb my own hair," he insisted.

Polk handed him the large ivory comb.

He jerked on the comb and couldn't find any place where it would slide through his hair. "I reckon I got some tangles."

"Your whole hair is one big tangle," Polk remarked.

"What am I goin' to do?"

Mrs. Lovelock continued to slice the onions. "Hold the roots with one hand and pull the comb through with the other."

"It ain't workin'," he grumbled.

"I can comb your hair," Polk insisted.

"You cannot. It's too tangled."

"Then you just keep tugging away until you're as bald as an egg."

Gabriel sighed and shoved the comb at her. "I can't believe I'm actually lettin' you do this."

Polk giggled. "Neither can I."

After twenty minutes of pain and apology, the hair was combed out.

And the onions sliced.

Mrs. Lovelock approached him, scissors in hand. "Now, my Gabe, how shall I cut this? I can just trim it up a little, or I can make you look very handsome."

Polk covered her mouth.

"Could I sort of get halfway to handsome?" Gabe murmured.

"Oh, I like that," Mrs. Lovelock grinned. "Halfway to handsome it is."

When she finally finished, an ankle-deep stack of hair littered the floor. She handed him a hand mirror.

"Halfway?" he moaned. "That's halfway to bein' bald."

"I decided my Gabe should be all the way handsome. Halfway just wasn't good enough." She turned to her daughter. "What do you think, Sissy?"

"It looks very nice, Mama."

"Thank you." Mrs. Lovelock laid down the scissors.

"But I liked it when it was long. I bet he won't let me comb it now," Polk complained.

"No, I won't. I reckon it'll look okay. I'll just keep my hat on."

"Your new hat," Mrs. Lovelock corrected.

"What do you mean?"

"There are new pony-rider boots and a hat in the bedroom, plus a new buckskin shirt and some wool trousers," she announced.

"Oh, no, I can't—"

"You have no choice, Gabriel Young. Yours got soaking wet while tending the station. Until yours dry out, you should wear station clothes. It goes with the job. The same would hold true for any station helper."

"If you put it that way."

A few minutes later he emerged with the new clothes, boots, and hat.

"Oh, my, doesn't he look handsome?" Mrs. Lovelock sighed. "He could put Johnny Frey to shame."

"Who's Johnny Frey?" Gabriel asked.

"He's a pony-rider in St. Joseph that is so handsome, rumor has it the girls line the roadway to throw petals in his path and hand him cookies and cakes," Mrs. Lovelock reported.

"I don't reckon I believe that," he said.

"Neither do I," Polk added. "But you do look very nice."

"I'd better go help out back before I blush to death." He pulled off his hat and ran his fingers through his short hair. "My hair has covered my ears for so long that I forgot how peculiar they look."

"They aren't peculiar," Polk protested. "A little large maybe, but not peculiar."

The sun blazed from a cloudless November sky. By 10:00 A.M. a $400 horse named Rachel was saddled and stood ready near the platform that was built for rapid transfer of rider and saddle. Polk had the food sack ready. They all practiced the transfer with Gabriel standing in for the pony-rider.

Polk decorated the corral with red, white, and blue ribbons. She and Gabriel sat at the front of the station and watched the western horizon for signs of the oncoming rider. "Daddy says he won't kick up any dust in this mud. That doesn't give us much lead time."

"What time does he usually come through?" Gabriel asked.

"We never know for sure, but on this special run they told us to be ready by 10:00 A.M. and that he would surely be here by 3:00 P.M."

"That's five hours difference."

"There are hindrances along the way," she remarked.

"Where is the home station to the east?"

"On the other side of the mountains. He comes right through that northern pass." She pointed.

"And how about west? Where does he go in that direction?"

"He rides forty-five more miles. But there are two swing stations before the home station."

"That sounds like a long ride for anyone."

"Yes, but the ponies are heroes too. They know the whole route. One time Terrance Lathey got shot off his horse, but the horse finished the run. The mail went on."

"How about Lathey?"

"He retired."

"Alive?"

She slugged him in the arm. "Of course he was alive. Dead people don't retire."

"So we could be sittin' out here for five hours?"

"You don't have to sit with me if you don't want to, Gabriel Young."

"I didn't say I didn't want to."

"So you do want to sit with me?"

"I didn't say that either."

"Then make up your mind."

Mr. Lovelock tramped around to the front. "Son, come back here and ride Rachel around the yard a bit."

"The $400 horse?"

"She's gettin' nervous tied to that post. Let's keep her legs limber. I don't want her to stiffen up. Darlin', you watch for . . ."

Gabriel glanced back at her. "You were wrong. I didn't have to make up my mind."

Polk stuck out her tongue.

They ate a bite of dinner at straight up noon but took it out in front of the station so they could watch the eastern trail. Gabriel was dozing on the step with the taste of black bread pudding still in his mouth when Polk shouted, "Here he comes! Here he comes!"

They sprinted to their positions as the horse limped into the station and Robert Chester Michaels staggered off.

"What happened, Bob?" Mr. Lovelock called as he yanked the mochila and slapped it on Rachel's back.

The pony-rider's shoulder slumped. "That storm brought an avalanche of boulders right down on my horse and me. The horse is lame."

"What happened to your shoulder?" Mrs. Lovelock asked.

"It must have gotten separated. You got to snap it back into place, Trent."

Mr. Lovelock hurried around behind him. "Mama, help me. Hold that left hand down."

"I can't watch this." Polk ran to the barn.

Mr. Lovelock shoved a glove into Robert Chester Michaels's mouth. "This is goin' to hurt a tad."

Gabriel's gaze froze on the man's drooping shoulder. Mr. Lovelock grunted and snapped the shoulder back.

The pony-rider didn't say a word.

Gabriel shook his head. *He may be the toughest man I ever saw in my life.*

Michaels spat the glove out.

"Who won the election?" Mrs. Lovelock asked.

"Mr. Lincoln was elected president, and the Southern states is pulling out!" Robert Chester Michaels shoved one foot into the stirrup, got halfway in the air . . . and passed out on the platform.

Mr. Lovelock hollered, "Get the smelling salts."

"He can't ride," Mrs. Lovelock cried out.

Trent Lovelock kneeled over the unconscious pony-rider. "But California has got to know. It's crucial that California knows!"

Gabriel flung himself into the saddle of the prancing mare. "I can make the ride."

"You don't know the way," Mrs. Lovelock shouted.

"Polk said the horse knows. I'll just follow!" Gabe grabbed the saddle horn as the horse bolted out of the station yard.

TEN

Gabriel and the $400 horse thundered across the Great Basin of northern Nevada, following a trail that led toward the treeless mountains in the west. The chestnut mare stretched her legs and began to fly. He felt the flat saddle slap against his rear and the front brim of his slouch hat turn up in the wind.

It's been a long time since I raced a horse. Big Boy ain't felt strong enough to run for weeks, and he could only gallop this fast in his dreams. Don't reckon I ever rode this fine a horse. I'll be sore after two hours at this clip, but what could I do? There was no one else to make the run.

The high desert was brown mud, but Gabriel was surprised that it had already dried enough to give the horse traction. Not much mud flew off Rachel's hooves. The wet ground softened the sound of hooves to a steady, rhythmic, dull pounding.

The stirrups are set too short for me. Robert Chester Michaels is a short man. I ain't short, but I'm skinny. Mama Lovelock will change that, I reckon. Now, Lord, I ain't dumb. I know that when she looks at me with them misty eyes, she ain't seein' Gabe Young. She's seein' them babies of hers that she lost and the little boy that died before Polk was born. But I figure that she needs to share that love, and You know that I surely ain't had a whole lot in the past years. So I figure You brought us together to help each other out.

The trail was well worn by previous pony-riders. About five feet wide on the flats, it snaked between sage and occasional boulders. Three miles out from the station, it turned south to avoid a huge expanse of low-lying lava rock.

I reckon that cave is out there. Maybe Fergus is still in it. On the other hand, they might be on the trail, and I'll come up on them. Pony-riders must see that sort of thing all the time. I wonder what it takes to sign on permanent. Course, if I was eatin' regular, I'd be too heavy for these little horses. And I wouldn't get to stay ever' night at Humboldt Flats. I reckon, I'll just be assistant station tender so I can hang around the Lovelocks, as long as they let me. It won't last forever, of course. Nothin' good ever does for me. But I can enjoy each and ever' day.

With his backside slapping leather, Gabriel leaned forward over the saddle horn to lower his profile. The gray-green sagebrush got smaller as he rode west. In some places it had disappeared. Most of the desert grass, where there was any, was short and a buckskin brown color.

They called me a hero, said I saved Mr. Lovelock's life. Don't know about that for sure. If I hadn't been there, he might have grabbed the oats and left the hay, and the mountain lion would never have attacked. So who's to say? But one thing's certain, they saved my life.

Gabriel kicked his feet out of the short stirrups and let his legs hang down. The burning in his knees faded as he stretched his legs. The trail dipped into a dry, sandy creek bed and then took a sharp right turn. He threw himself against the horse's neck and held on. He felt the warmth of the horse's hair and the beat of her heart.

If Polk hadn't disobeyed her daddy and rode over the rise to the north, if she hadn't found me there . . . Oh, Lord, there's no tellin' how much longer I would have lasted. At that point I didn't even care.

The sunlight was just far enough ahead of them that Gabriel could see no shadows. He shoved his hat down tighter and adjusted the little cloth grub sack strapped over the saddle horn. He thought about the sweet taste of white gravy over Mama Lovelock's flaky biscuits.

But now, Lord, I have things to live for. A person needs things to live for. People to live for. I know the Lovelocks some, and I'd like to know them better.

At the western edge of Humboldt Flats, the trail turned up into the hills. The horse slowed a little as they hit the incline. He jammed his boots back into the stirrups, but continued to lean forward over the saddle horn. The air, no longer filled with the scent of sage, grew colder and the trail steeper.

And I reckon I know You some now 'cause I truly do believe all that I read about Jesus. I'd like to know You better too.

A faint trail branched off to the south, but the mare kept on the wider one. Soon they came to a narrow pass in the rocks. He was afraid his feet would drag on the granite, but the horse never slowed. In a flash he was through the pass and galloping down the slope.

I reckon that trail to the south avoided the pass. I surmise there are times to change the trail. I wonder how they know when to change trails? Same is true in life, I suppose. In just a couple days, it all begins to make sense. My life ain't never made sense before. But I don't know exactly what I'm doin' ridin' across a trail I've never taken.

When they broke through the hills into another broad, flat valley, he expected something different, but it was identical to Humboldt Flats—scattered low sage, very little brown grass, and nothing else in sight.

Maybe that's my whole life, Lord. Ridin' across a trail I've never taken. Good thing this pony knows the way.

He dropped his left boot from the stirrup and rubbed his knee. When he sat up, he could feel the saddle pound into his rear. He searched for a more comfortable position but ended up leaning low over the saddle horn again.

This is goin' to be a long day. I guess I ride to the home station before we change. Of course, if any of the stations has a regular pony-rider, he can take over. I must have gone five miles already. Maybe more. Have we been gone an hour? If Rachel could talk, she could tell me how much farther. Wait a minute. This is a new horse. She was brought in for the election run. She don't know this route. What am I thinkin'? I have no idea where I'm goin'. I don't even know the name of the next station. It's just fifteen miles down the trail.

Gabe spotted a wide trail leading to the south of the mountain range, but he couldn't see any traffic on it.

That's the old immigrant trail. But what trail am I supposed to follow? I could keep on this one until I get lost or confused. I have no idea what I'll do then.

Gabriel rocked back and forth in the saddle in tune with the gait of the galloping horse. He stared down at the little grub sack but didn't take anything out.

I can't believe this. I get my life turned around and then ride out into the wilderness.

To the north he spotted a pronghorn antelope spying them out. When Rachel thundered up the next draw, Gabriel found himself in the middle of two hundred startled antelope, which bolted and ran alongside of them. After several hundred yards, the antelope veered to the north.

If they had stayed with us, they would have masked the trail. I ain't never rode with antelopes before. Okay, Lord, I didn't turn my life around any more than I turned those antelopes. You turned my life around. I ain't been down this trail, and neither has this pony. But You have. You lead and I'll follow. But I ain't never tried that before.

Gabriel watched the trail ahead as it approached another mountain. It was a long, lone butte covered with jagged granite rock. There was no vegetation, but he did spot dark shadows on the northern slope.

There's a whole lot of things I ain't never done before.

At the base of the mountain were three trails. One went north around the butte. A second veered to the south around the butte. The third seemed to head straight up the mountain.

Gabriel hesitated.

Rachel didn't.

She dug in her hooves and plowed straight up the mountain.

I can't believe the right trail is the steepest, but then there's no reason for this trail unless it's the right one. She's goin' to wear herself out. This pony has heart. I ain't never seen a horse with more try. I reckon over this mountain we'll see the next station. None too soon for both of us.

The butte proved deceptive in size. Once they reached what Gabriel thought would be the pinnacle, a higher ridge stretched beyond them. They rode several miles still climbing the mountain. As they approached a pass through the rocks, he spotted a thin coil of smoke from a campfire.

Someone's up on this mountain? Several of them. Indians. Fergus, no doubt. I can't stop and visit. I've got to keep goin'. Hope they understand. I can at least wave. I don't remember them havin' that many horses. Maybe they kept the horses back out on the Flats.

As he approached, he could see several people scurry around. Some seemed to be hiding.

They're a shy bunch. There's no reason to hide from me. I don't even have a gun. All the pony-riders have guns, but I was sort of in a hurry. That Indian man has a gun. He's better off than I am.

"Let's impress them with what a fine horse you are, girl." He kicked her flanks. "Show them your speed." He pulled off his hat and waved it in front of him.

The Indian to his right raised the musket to his shoulder.

That ain't Fergus.

And he's aiming that gun at me!

Gabe ducked his head and shoulders toward the horse's neck and yanked down his hat-waving arm just as he heard an explosion. The horse roared right through the Indian encampment. He could feel his heart thump in his temples as several more shots rang out.

There really are Paiutes on the prowl! That was a war party. They'll come after me. At least the trail is downhill for a while.

Gabriel glanced over his shoulder but could see no

one in pursuit. He raised his hat to jam it back on his head. He felt a round hole the size of his thumb in the front brim.

That close? I came that close to endin' my life? Am I goin' to die today, Lord? Are You goin' to give me a wonderful family and then take them away just like that?

I guess that sounds ungrateful. Grandma used to sing a song about the joys of heaven. So I reckon it will be better than what we got here. But, still, I'd like a little more time down here for comparison, if You don't mind.

Gabe jammed the hat down to his ears and glanced over his shoulder again. He could see no one giving chase.

But on the other side of the flat valley, a wavy column of smoke divided the horizon between north and south.

"That's it, girl. That's the next station. They got a fire in the fireplace waitin' for us. If I had a bugle, I'd toot it. We're goin' to make it. Let's roar in there and get this election news to California."

They dashed across the flat desert. Gabriel pressed his head to the horse's neck to keep the lowest profile. When he sat back up, they were only a mile from the column of smoke.

They—they—they burned the station. . . . It ain't the fireplace. . . . It's the whole buildin'.

When they reached the ashes of the station, Gabriel reined up for the first time since leaving Humboldt Flats. He glanced back at the mountain but saw no one in pursuit.

Gabe slipped to the ground and staggered as his weight hit his knees. His rear end felt sore and stiff. He led the horse over to the smoldering building.

"They stole the horses and burned it to the ground,

girl. Where's the station tender? Oh, Lord, have mercy on his soul—and ours."

He led the labored horse around the building. "Hey!" he hollered. "Are you out there?"

What am I supposed to do now? Do I look for the station man . . . or his body? Do I go back? I can't go back. California has to hear. I'll go on.

He pulled himself back up into the saddle. "We have to do it again, Rachel. I'm sorry. We got to get these letters to the next station." He scooped a handful of oats out of the little cloth sack and jammed them into the horse's mouth. He rode her to the wooden water trough next to the springs.

"This is the only wooden item they didn't burn." Gabe let her have a short drink, then rode her back out on the trail. "Fifteen more miles, girl. Somehow you got to find it in you."

The trail sloped to the southwest and looked flat and barren for fifty miles.

Rachel found a pace she could sustain as Gabriel kept her steady, always glancing back over his shoulder.

I don't know what I'd do if they came after me. Try to outrun them, I reckon. I surely don't know how far this pony can gallop, but I suppose I'll find out. Nothin' is ever as simple as it seems. I was just goin' to ride a few miles. Well, I guess I knew I had to ride until I found a relief rider.

But I surely didn't know I was ridin' for my life.

The afternoon stretched on. Sweat dribbled down the inside of Gabriel's buckskin shirt. His knees burned. His rear was numb, his throat full of dirt, lips chapped.

They had just leaped a ten-foot-deep dry creek bed when he spotted trees and a cabin.

"There it is! It ain't burnt. That's the next station, girl. I don't know if they want me to ride on, but at least you'll get to rest! There's a horse out front. That must be the relay. We made it, girl."

Gabriel galloped to the front door of the cabin as a short man stepped out on the front porch pointing a revolver. "Who in blazes are you?" he hollered.

Gabriel leaped down and led Rachel to the step. "I'm Gabe Young. I'm helpin' Mr. Lovelock over at Humboldt Flats. Mr. Michaels dislocated his shoulder and couldn't ride, and I filled in. What's goin' on here?"

"McKenna's inside and shot. The Paiutes are on the prowl again. They stole the horses from here."

"What are we goin' to do?"

"You got the westbound mail?"

"Yes, sir."

"Did Lincoln win?" the man asked.

"Yes, sir, and the South said they're going to secede."

"Well, I'll swan. There's goin' to be a war, boy. Lord help us, there's goin' to be a war. Help me load McKenna on my horse. We'll take him west with us. Can that pony make another fifteen miles?"

"Not if I push her too much. She came all the way from Humboldt Flats."

"You didn't change at Cold Springs?"

"Cold Springs is burnt to the ground. There was a party of Paiutes on the mountain east of there. They had the horses."

"It's burnt? How about Pop Baynard?"

"I couldn't find anyone."

"That does it. They'll close the route."

"What?"

"The Pony Express with be closed until the army can open up the route. It's a good thing you got through."

"What about the Lovelocks at Humboldt Flats? If the Paiutes are movin' that way, aren't they in the line of destruction?"

"Can't be helped, boy. The best thing we can do is get McKenna to the home station and this mail on to California."

"But—but—I can't leave them out there."

"Are they your kin?"

"Eh, yes . . . yes, they are. They're my family." Gabriel pulled the mochila off his saddle and shoved it at the man. "You take the mail. I'm goin' back."

"You really goin' to try and make it?"

"I have to make it," Gabriel mumbled.

"I've got the eastbound mail right here. You might as well carry it," the man said. "It's a cinch I'm not goin' out there."

Gabriel slapped the eastbound mochila onto his saddle and grabbed another handful of oats for Rachel out of the cotton feed sack and led her to the water trough. He washed his face and took a quick drink. Then he helped load McKenna onto the pony-rider's horse.

"Good luck, son. You're a braver man than me." He trotted the horse southwest. "So Lincoln won. Well, I reckon that means tough times up ahead for the country."

Gabriel watched them disappear over the rise. He kicked Rachel's flanks and bolted back up the trail he had just come down.

If I don't get back to Humboldt Flats before that band of Paiutes, it don't matter what happens to the rest of the country.

ELEVEN

The return trip to the burned-out swing station at Cold Springs did not seem as long to Gabriel, but he didn't know why.

The Great Basin of Nevada didn't change.

There was no less sage.

No less wind.

No fewer people.

It was empty and a gradual uphill climb. He let Rachel lope along, and she seemed to enjoy the slower pace. But his mind raced through the miles.

If they attacked McKenna's Station first and then Cold Springs, that means they will attack Humboldt Flats. Maybe they're there already, but that's a possibility I can't bear to ponder. They were camped at the pass. Maybe they won't go east until tomorrow.

Lord, how far will they go until they have enough horses? They'll stop somewhere, won't they?

The sun slipped behind the mountain at Cold Springs, but the acrid smell of the smoldering building lingered. This time when Gabriel slid to the ground, his knees gave out. He tumbled to his hands and knees.

"You're better at this than I am, girl." He led the

horse to the water trough. "A $400 horse and a four-bit rider. We're a pair."

Gabriel washed his face and fed the horse the rest of the oats. He stared at the grub bag. "I should probably eat somethin' myself, but my stomach is in a knot. I'd probably lose it and make a big mess over both of us. Besides, if you get weak, I'll see if you'll eat one of Mama Lovelock's biscuits."

His legs were so stiff he had to yank his boot up into the stirrup with his hand as he crawled back onto the saddle. He reset his hat, heaved a big sigh, and kicked the horse in the flanks.

They roared off to the east and the big lone mountain that stood between them and Humboldt Flats. They raced the shadows across the basin floor for over thirty minutes.

And lost.

By the time they approached the base of the big butte, twilight had settled in, and even the sage blurred in his vision.

Now, Lord, I've got to decide. There's a trail around this mountain to the south and another to the north. They are longer than the one over the top but safer. If I come across the Paiutes, I could try to outrun them out onto the desert. They were camped up on top of this pass; so I shouldn't go back that way.

But if they're movin' toward Humboldt Flats or are already there, the long trail won't do me any good.

If I go around the mountain, I'm no help to the Lovelocks if they're in trouble. If I plow over the top, and the Paiutes are still there, I'll get ambushed. There's no surprise left. Lord, I'm new to this prayin', but I reckon You know what I should do. If You'll just give me a sign . . . maybe have an antelope run up the trail that You want me to go on. Just a word. Just a poke. Just a little help.

He pulled up and stopped where the trail forked.

Rachel danced from side to side and glanced back at him. "I know, girl. You want to keep goin' too. I'm waitin' for a word from the Lord. Did you ever wait for a word from the Lord?"

Am I talkin' spiritual to my horse?

Lord, I can't wait. You've got to show me. Now.

If I go around the mountain and save my life, and yet the Lovelocks lose theirs, I could never live with that. If I go over the top and lose my life . . . well . . . at least I'll have no regrets. And if they lose their lives today, I imagine we'll all hike into heaven together. And that won't be so bad. Mama Lovelock can introduce me around.

"We're goin' over the top, girl, and may the Lord have mercy on all of us."

Gabriel strained in the dying twilight to scout the trail ahead of them. The slope up the west side of the mountain was more gradual than that on the east. The horse kept a steady pace, though her chest and neck were lathered white with sweat.

Now, Lord, I don't know why You didn't answer me down there. It would have been a good time for a voice from heaven to say, "Go south," or somethin' like that. It's like You led me to the mountain and then made me make up my own mind. What kind of leadin' is that? Except, I reckon . . . You could just slip a thought of Your own in my mind, couldn't You? I don't know how this leadin' works, but You know my heart. And I tried. I truly did try to let You lead, but I had to get movin'.

It was almost dark when they crested the pass. Gabriel pulled out his big knife and bit the handle.

I've never knife-fought a man before, but I've watched plenty of others do it. I'll fight to the death to survive. I surely would like another hug from Mama Lovelock before I go.

The Paiutes will fight to the death too. I don't blame 'em, Lord. I imagine they're doin' what they think they ought to do. And I'm doin' what I think I ought to do. I wonder if either of us got it right?

He had just squeezed through the narrow boulders when he spotted the campfires.

"They're still here, girl! They haven't gone to Humboldt Flats! That's good . . . I think."

He saw the flash of powder, the report of the muskets, and could hear bullets buzz like hornets. Indians were shouting on all sides of him, and they scurried out of his way as he galloped through camp.

He shouted back. At the top of his voice, Gabriel Young hollered and screamed.

With another flash from a gun, he could see in the dying daylight a Paiute warrior on the bluff on the east side of the encampment. The Indian brandished a huge knife.

He's going to jump me, and I can't do anything about it. If I turn around, I'm lost for sure. If I throw my knife and miss, I won't have anythin' to fight him with when I fall off the horse.

If I had a rock I could . . .

Gabriel plucked the cotton food sack off the saddle horn, whipped it around and around over his head, and hurled it at the waiting Indian.

Another blast from a gun lit up the night, and he saw the sack strike the Indian in the face. The warrior tumbled backward into the night.

Gabriel and Rachel roared past the bluff.

Mama Lovelock, it looks like your biscuits saved your Gabe!

The trail was now completely dark. He gave the horse rein and let her lead. Several times he thought he heard hoofbeats behind him, but he had no way of knowing. He kept the knife in his mouth and leaned across the horse's neck.

I don't know if I'm on the right trail. In such a dark night I don't even know if I'm on a trail at all. If we stumble into the lava beds, we'll both go down hard. If we veer too far south, we'll miss Humboldt Flats.

But Big Boy found it for me. Rachel can find it too. That was just two nights ago. My head is still spinnin', Lord. I kept expectin' to wake up on the dirt in some minin' camp, sloppin' buckets and tendin' fires. If these two days have been a dream, well, I'm proud of myself 'cause I didn't know I could dream so good.

But them tears in Mama Lovelock's eyes weren't no dream. We just got to find the station and see what happens next. Whatever is up ahead can't be as bad as what's behind.

In my life.

And in this night.

Rachel slowed, and Gabriel didn't push her.

The Nevada stars were bright, but there was no moon. The air was cold but tolerable. Gabriel could make out some larger sagebrush and boulders. He found it didn't matter if he closed his eyes or opened them, the horse followed the same trail at the same speed. He shoved the knife back into the scabbard in his boot.

With his eyes closed, he rested his chin on his chest.

Fifteen miles to Cold Springs. Fifteen miles to McKenna's. That's thirty miles out and thirty miles back. That's about normal for a pony-rider's day. But I ain't done that much hard ridin' in my whole life tied together. The only good thing about never havin' anyplace to go is that I was never in a hurry to get there.

Now I'm in a hurry.

Not just for the mail.

But to get home.

Lord, that has to be just about the sweetest word ever invented.

Home.

Ever'one has to have a home.

When Gabriel opened his eyes, they were parked out on the desert.

"What's the matter, girl? Did you go to sleep too?" he whispered.

He studied the night sky. A sliver of a moon had popped up in the east, and he could see dark shadows like trees about 300 yards in the distance.

"That's it, girl, you found . . ." Gabriel's words died when he spied campfires around the station and corrals.

Paiutes! It must be another band. They got it surrounded. And there's no shootin'. It's all over. We're too late. No. *This isn't right. This is not the way it's goin' to be. No, Lord. You can't do this to me. I tried too hard. I did everything right. It's supposed to be me who dies. Nobody would care if I was gone.*

Except Mama Lovelock.

Maybe someone's still alive!

"Come on, Rachel, we're ridin' in proud 'cause this is my last ride if they're all dead."

He kicked her flanks and was surprised that the mare had a another burst of speed in her as they galloped toward the campfires.

When he thundered closer, he thought he saw a man with a blue coat near the fire closest to the back door of the house. He reined up quickly.

A voice shouted, "Halt and identify!"

"What?" he croaked.

"I said, 'halt and identify,' or I'll shoot you off that horse."

"Mr. Lovelock?"

"Sergeant Major Haughton. Identify yourself."

"Gabriel Young."

"You the pony-rider?"

"Yes, sir."

"Why didn't you say so? Pony-rider!" he shouted.

The relay was shouted from campfire to campfire. The back door swung open, and a barefoot Trent Lovelock ran out into the yard. Beside him jogged Robert Chester Michaels.

"Is it Dawson?" Michaels called out.

"No, sir, it's me, Gabe Young."

"Gabe! Mama! Your Gabe is here!" Mr. Lovelock shouted.

The soldiers gathered around him.

"You still ridin' Rachel? Didn't you make it through?"

"I made it. I got the mail to McKenna's, and that ol' boy took it west."

An officer buttoned his coat as he walked up to the fire. "We heard there was trouble west of here."

"Cold Springs is burnt to the ground. The horses and tender are gone. McKenna lost his horses but saved the station. He was wounded, and the eastbound pony-rider took him back to the home station. Paiutes are camped up on the mountain."

"They aren't bringing the eastbound mail?" Trent Lovelock asked.

"I brought it, Mr. Lovelock."

"You did?"

"Yes, sir."

"Then saddle me a pony, Trent. I'm takin' it on," Bob Michaels called out.

"What about your shoulder?" Gabriel asked.

"It will survive. I needed the rest, and you gave it to me. Not bad, son, for a day's work. I'll put you in for a bonus."

"I don't need no bonus," Gabriel protested.

"Son, nobody carries letters for Russell, Majors, and Waddell without gettin' paid."

Mr. Lovelock and Michaels ran to the corrals as one of the soldiers led a weary Rachel to the water trough.

"Gabe!"

Mrs. Lovelock stood in the lantern light at the back door in a flannel gown. "Is my Gabe out there?" she hollered.

His knees didn't burn.

His legs weren't stiff.

His rear felt just fine.

He sprinted to the back door and then paused in front of the step. Several soldiers lounged nearby.

Mrs. Lovelock glanced at the soldiers, then back at him. "Gabe Young, you had me worried to death. Stayin' out late like this. I didn't even know where you were."

"I'm sorry, Mama Lovelock. I didn't mean to worry you. I won't do it again."

"Now that's okay this time. Sissy, warm him up some supper. Don't just stand there. Come on in."

Mrs. Lovelock tugged him inside and closed the door. "I didn't want to embarrass you out there with the soldiers," she whispered.

Then she threw her arms around him and hugged.

By the time Gabriel made it outside the next morning, the soldiers had struck camp and headed west. Mr. Lovelock was rubbing down Rachel's legs with liniment. "Mornin', Mr. Young," he greeted.

"Howdy, Mr. Lovelock. Sorry I slept in."

"The sun is just comin' up. Looks like a beautiful day. I'm proud of you for makin' that trip. There probably aren't ten men in Nevada that could have done what you did."

"It just seemed like the right thing to do."

"Did you pray about it?"

"Yes, sir, I did."

"Did the Lord answer your prayers?"

"Yes, sir. I reckon He did."

"Mama says you can't join the pony-riders because she doesn't want to go through that anguish another time."

"Neither do I. I got great respect for those men. But I don't think I want to do it again."

"I think I'll keep Rachel and your Big Boy in the same pen for a while. They both need some rest."

"I reckon he'll enjoy havin' someone to talk to besides me," Gabe remarked. "What kind of chores can I do?"

"You can just rest up today, son."

"Mr. Lovelock, you know I can't do that any more than you can with your wounds."

Mr. Lovelock grinned and shook his head. "You got that right, son. Okay, you feed the horses in that second corral. Don't know when we'll need them, but we want to stand ready. Looks like you'll have some help." He pointed to the back door.

Polk emerged wearing a crisp yellow gingham dress and yellow bonnet. "Good morning, sleepy."

"Mornin', Polk. You surely look purdy. Did you dress up for the soldier boys?"

"No, I dressed up for the pony-boy."

"For me?"

She shook her head and sighed. "You need so much schooling, I don't know where to begin."

He started graining the horses, and she trailed behind.

"Did you like my biscuits?"

"I didn't have biscuits this mornin'."

"I mean yesterday. In the pony-rider sack. Those were my biscuits, you know. I don't think I used enough soda. Daddy said they were hard as rock when they got cold. He wouldn't eat them. Did you like them, Gabe?"

"Polk, them biscuits of yours were perfect."

"They were?"

"In fact, they were real lifesavers to me," he grinned.

"See? What does Daddy know?"

"Trent," Mrs. Lovelock called from the back door. "There's a visitor coming this way from the east."

Mr. Lovelock, Polk, and Gabriel hiked around to the

front of the station and waited as a bearded man on a horse approached.

"Mr. Davis," Gabe called out.

"Howdy, son. Howdy, Lovelock . . . and missy." He tipped his hat. "I just need to fill some water jugs. Is that all right?"

"Climb on down and make yourself at home," Mr. Lovelock offered. "Where's your partner?"

"He's holdin' down the claim until I file on it," Davis reported as he dismounted.

"Claim? You mean you found gold at Chocolate Butte?" Mr. Lovelock asked.

"Shoot, no. There ain't nothin' over there worth spit," he said.

Gabriel took the reins and led the prospector's horse as they all circled around behind the building.

"We was headin' back this way yesterday," Davis continued, "and late last evenin' over at the base of the Humboldts, we was comin' around a narrow trail, and the horses started pitchin' a fit. I grabbed my gun and hiked ahead to investigate."

"Was it Paiutes?" Polk asked.

"Paiutes? No, missy. A huge mountain lion sprawled across the trail just as dead as can be. He had a slash in his shoulder and probably bled to death. Paiutes did that all right. No one else gets close enough to a cat that size with only a knife."

Mr. Lovelock glanced over at Gabriel and nodded.

"Anyway, the horses weren't goin' to step over a big old cat even if he was dead. So I shoved him down into a gulch. I figured the smell is what touched off the horses;

so me and my partner covered him up with rocks and boulders. About dark we found it."

"Found what?" Gabriel asked.

"Gold, son. Right under them boulders I tossed on the cat was fine, sandy gold. We panned by candlelight until our water ran out. It looks mighty promisin'; so I'm takin' my pard back some water and will then head out and file a claim. We're goin' to call it the Slash Cat Diggin's. What do you think of that? If it hadn't been for that dead cat, I'd never have found the gold."

When they reached the back of the station, Everett Davis studied the layout. "Lovelock, I never could tend a station like this. Too sedentary. Too boring. I'd get cabin fever. Why, what's the last excitin' thing that happened around here?"

Mr. Lovelock laughed. "The pony-rider brought word of Mr. Lincoln's election."

"You see, that proves my point," Davis blustered. "If politics is the most excitin' thing, you're livin' a dull life. I'm happy you like it, but I need more excitement."

"Don't underestimate politics, Davis," Mr. Lovelock pressed. "Say, are you related to Jefferson Davis in . . ."

Polk grabbed Gabriel's hand.

"What're you doin'?" he whispered.

She slipped her fingers into his. "I'm savin' you from a windy conversation about politics."

"But I've got chores to do," he protested as she tugged him toward the barn.

"Yes, you do, Gabe Young. And I intend to watch you do them."

Gabriel noticed once more that her nose and ears wiggled at the same time when she smiled.

For a list of other books
by this author, write:
Stephen Bly
Winchester, Idaho 83555,
or check out his website:
www.blybooks.com